HUMAN RESOURCES

stories

Josh Goldfaden

Tin House Books

*For my mother and the generosity, clarity,
and absurdity of her belief in me.*

■

Published by Tin House Books,
Portland, Oregon, and New York, New York
Distributed to the trade by Publishers Group West,
1700 Fourth St., Berkeley, CA 94710, www.pgw.com

Library of Congress Cataloging-in-Publication Data

Goldfaden, Josh, 1972–
Human resources : stories / Josh Goldfaden.—1st U.S. ed.
p. cm.
ISBN 978-0-9776989-1-2
I. Title.
PS3607.O4535H86 2006
813'.6—dc22
2006100130

First U.S. edition 2007

ISBN 10: 0-9776989-1-2

Designed by Pauline Neuwirth, Neuwirth & Associates, Inc.

www.tinhouse.com
Printed in Canada

These stories have appeared, in slightly different form, in the following
publications: "King of the Ferns" in *Chelsea*; "The Veronese Circle" in
New England Review; "Maryville, California, Pop. 7" in *Meridian*; "Disorder
Destroyers" in *Mid-American Review*; "Documentary" in *Salmagundi*; "Looking at
Animals" in the *Sewanee Review*; "Nautical Intervention" in ZYZZYVA;
"Top of the List" in *Painted Bride Quarterly*.

CONTENTS

THE
VERONESE CIRCLE

THE TRAIN TO Granada takes eleven hours, which is long enough for Eli, all deranged on ouzo, to threaten to jump off the train, proclaiming he's "more worthless than this chicken wing." Apparently he'd found the chicken in one of the trash bins he and Beatrice had been digging through, trying to prove their theory that riches prefer meek and filthy terrain. Dr. and Mrs. Doveman talk him out of jumping by explaining how Duchamp proved self-worth wasn't worth all that much when you got right down to it. Tragedy averted, Eli still has time to climb into Sharini's couchette—the only girl he hasn't fucked loudly and tearfully—and fuck her loudly and tearfully.

On the train station platform, Mrs. Doveman counts the writers to make sure they're all accounted for. As the au pair, I stand aside, holding her son, Camus, who's sleeping peacefully, and though it's only eight in the morning, my arms and chest grow damp under the Spanish summer heat and Camus' small body.

"Where's Helene?" Mrs. Doveman asks.

"'Gone and never coming / back / Taken by hellhound bakers to / feast on loaves: / tepid shit-bread,'" Beatrice says. "It's from the Pindaric ode I'm working on."

"Very powerful," Mrs. Doveman says. "Positively visceral."

It was the same in Verona, the same in Paris, and will no doubt continue throughout the trip; the writers are always wandering off, and though they'll discuss Helene's possible whereabouts, motives for her disappearance, her menstrual cycle, her abandonment issues, it will get them nowhere and she'll be back in about an hour. I take my career book, *After College . . . What?*, and Camus, and wait on a nearby bench. The book tells me, "In Man's long process of development, we have come up with things to do which we call 'occupations,' and without them we would be miserable, for Man is an active creature."

Occupation #1: Accordion Maker.

Each of the six writers (there were seven until, in Paris, Niles found out that Victor Hugo's former apartment was for rent and told Dr. Doveman, "Goddamnit, man, the fates are practically begging to suck me off! I have to let them!") paid the Dovemans thirty-five hundred dollars for this four-week traveling writer's colony from Verona to Paris to Granada to Casablanca to Krakow to Prague to

Istanbul and finally back to Verona. Dr. Doveman calls it the Veronese Circle.

At our orientation, in the courtyard of what is believed to be Juliet's home, Dr. Doveman groped a bronze statue of Juliet, made out with the pure Veronese soil, and said, "Let Verona cradle you like some benevolent Ur-Mother, as it cradled Romeo and Juliet—and let their story color the writing all of you will generate during the next twenty-eight days." Then he wiped the dirt from his lips and pawed at a real Veronese boulder, upon which, he claimed, "Romeo may once have sat, grief stricken."

Seven years ago, Dr. Doveman's first and only novel, *Romeo and Julio*, a bisexual rewriting of Shakespeare's classic, caught hold of a particularly carnal zeitgeist and inexplicably topped the bestseller list. Mrs. Doveman is an unpublished poet with a remarkable memory for every positive review Dr. Doveman ever received. She's working on a manuscript of poems constructed from lines of these reviews.

Helene strolls back two hours later. She'd been observing a dubious (her word) couple on the train and "knew that under no circumstances could I allow them to escape my searching gaze." She followed them off the train, around a fruit market, and then watched them drink coffee and eat egg sandwiches. She's recorded some of their dialogue and is pretty excited to read it to the others, and they're pretty excited to hear it, and there would probably be an impromptu reading right here on the train station platform if Dr. Doveman didn't announce, "All this erudite voyeurism is fine and dandy, yet there is balderdash, damn me, and that balderdash is our engagement at the university for which we are unforgivably late, goddamn me to hell, so, my budding geniuses, as Romeo said, act 1, scene 5, 'Direct my sail!—On, lusty gentlemen!'"

And we walk. Hundred-degree heat, hauling fifty-pound backpacks, and we walk. Dr. Doveman brainwashed the writers to believe you can't taste the lives of *the other* in taxicabs, so no one complains. I say, "Hey, you guys, what if we tasted the life of a cabdriver? Do they qualify as 'the other'?"

"Did somebody speak?" Mrs. Doveman says. "I heard something like a rat twittering about."

I'm still not used to being treated as subhuman. I'm probably not a budding genius, but I'm still basically worthy. To them, though, I'm just the lowly au pair boy, and as long as Camus and I are quiet, they're pleased to ignore us both.

I took this job despite the fact that the summer camp where I've worked for the past three summers offered me the choicest camp assignments, like s'mores supervisor and official campfire storyteller—even suggested I start up that lake snorkeling program I've been pushing for the past two years. The thing is, I'd just graduated from college. If I took the same old job, what was to stop me from becoming one of those camp-counselor lifers with the terrible ponytail and rank Birkenstocks? I needed a vocation, and until I found one, au pairing seemed a good compromise: a sort of jet-setting camp counselor.

We walk for far too long and I'm shocked when Mrs. Doveman takes Camus from my arms, cooing, "There's my baby."

"I'm not a baby," he says, "and I don't like you today."

Dr. and Mrs. Doveman are of the school of parenting wherein you put huge amounts of pressure on the kid but otherwise ignore him, and when you ultimately fail at your own life, you always have his life and his potential to fall back on. In the rare moments when he's playing like a normal kid, they ask him whether he thinks Tolstoy spent *his* time bouncing a ball against the floor, coloring pictures of anatomically incorrect horses, or stacking dirt on top of other dirt. "Go do something great," they'll order, and he'll look to me, perplexed, his dirt not just dirt after all, but a rocky castle fortress with mud-clump guards and pebbled towers, and he'll look from me back to the fortress, unsure of how to do something great, unsure what something great would even look like, but positive that his dirt fortress isn't it—so he'll stand and kick it over, and smash it back into dirt.

Mrs. Doveman awkwardly cuddles Camus for a few moments before handing him back to me, complaining he's moist and a bit gluey. Through it all, Michaelangelo talks at me again about how his agent insists he's "*the* voice of a disenfranchised generation." I congratulate him and he does his best to appear humble, but gladdened. Then he asks if

I've heard about the cutthroat industry battle to purchase his screenplay. I have.

Camus and I share a dorm room with Olivier, a brooding poet who's far too self-involved to be bothered if Camus cries out in the night, which he often does. I ask him if he wouldn't mind watching Camus while I shower and he says that the heroic couplets he's working on are only on the verge of answering the question of why we are here. "Go ahead and shower, Ted, certainly the oldest and most fundamental of questions can wait while you wash your useless body and my talents are squandered watching a six-year-old."

"Seven," Camus cries. "Goddamnit, seven."

"Tell me about the couplets," I say.

"You wouldn't understand," Olivier says. He looks me over (bitter distaste), his vanity eventually winning out over my abject non-writer status. "Okay," he says. "Try. To. Follow. Along. Think of Whitman, in his poem 'I Am the Poet,' when he says 'all the things seen are real.' It's a poetic truth, and I'm close, Ted, I'm brutally close to discovering an even greater truth: something that can tell us why the things we see are real, and even more importantly, what value we have in relation to these things—what the value is of a single human life!

"I can see by your bewildered gape that you have no conception of what I'm talking about. I'm talking about why Eli made the right decision not to throw himself off that train. If I write this as well as I think I can, it'll answer that question."

"I understand," I say.

"I doubt it. Now go and rinse away your filth."

Occupation #81: Diplomat.

"Okay," I say brightly, "I will."

Camus is sprawled out on my bed with a book of Yeats, and I lie down next to him. "Do you need anything, buddy?" He shakes his head and smiles. "Be good for Unkie Olivier," I say. He smiles again and holds up a middle finger, a gesture he's just learned and can probably no more understand than the book of poetry he's pretending to read.

In the shower, I think about Camus—how sweet but fucked-up he is, and what it would take to fix him. *After College . . . What?* suggests itemizing one's talents in order to find "your own harmonious vocation." I know probably two hundred camp songs and can start a fire with wet wood. I know glassblowing, wallet making, all the basic sailing knots, and I can execute an Eskimo roll in either a sea or a river kayak. In just two lessons, I can train almost any kid to be an adequate archer. I'm not sure, however, if any of these skills can help Camus.

"You are chock-full of talents," the book assures me, "if only you'll allow yourself to see them." It recommends I stand in front of a mirror and frankly appraise what I see. In the shower-misted mirror, my reflection: pale bellied, fat-cheeked, lethargic balls, misshapen freckles covering sunken, hairy shoulders. But there's also a strong, rocky cliff of a chin, eyes so blue the fogged-up mirror does nothing to dull them, and forearms any sailor would be proud to have. It's a reflection that, given the chance, could be capable of quite a bit.

When I get out of the shower, Olivier, face down on the desk, is weeping quietly, "Where are you, my beautiful muse?" and Camus is setting fire to my blanket with Olivier's matches. I stomp on the smoldering blanket. When it's mostly out, I switch it with Olivier's. He's far too absorbed in his failure to answer the unanswerable to care about a char-crusted blanket. The air is lush with burning blanket and Olivier's chain-smoking. Olivier, still face down, mutters weakly, "I am lost. Fetch me my Rilke."

Later, we all go to the workshop. There's our writers and the usual special guest, in this case a pole-shaped Spanish poet. It's the same as all the workshops in all the cities before. They discuss writing schedules—is it better to write in the morning or the afternoon? Is it true that Rimbaud only wrote in the middle of the night?—Beatrice reads another poem about her dead boyfriend and begins weeping during the last line, which is "Now you're dead. Now you're dead. Now you're dead!" Eli reads a chapter from his novel about a writer who hates himself too much to give himself the pleasure of suicide (all the girls and Dr. Doveman swoon). Helene reads an impenetrable villanelle about a solitary cup of soup that learns to love, and then Sharini, as always, reads a poem so clearly better than everyone else's that it's embarrassing to listen to. She's our beautiful, angry, talented one, and all the others want equally to fuck and to kill her. Then they all compliment each other using words like "enchanting" and "genius," and the pole-shaped Spanish poet assures us that "there is nowhere in God's robust world I would rather be than right here critiquing this most misguided work," and he laughs though no one else does.

Michaelangelo sits beside me making one-word comments about each of the readers: *Banal. Asinine. Pestilent. Folly.* He himself refuses to read in public, claiming the material that would have made up his first book was "filched in bits and pieces by the sort of hack writers who frequent readings." Through it all, I keep Camus occupied by letting him burn the bottom of his desk with a lighter he's stolen from somewhere.

Eventually, Dr. Doveman, always making light of both his alcoholism and sweating condition, suggests, "What say we slip out of these wet clothes and into a dry martini?" Sometimes Dr. and Mrs. Doveman invite me along if there's something they want Camus to see, like a bar where a famous writer once drank himself to death, but apparently there's no such richness in Granada's bar scene, and Mrs. Doveman kisses Camus on the cheek (purple lipped, scent of wine), hands him a stack of *pesetas* and tells me to take good care of her future Pulitzer Prize winner. I take one last look at the writers—so lamenting and wounded and full of praise for each other—and I'm a little jealous. We're *almost* the same: so midtwenties, so American, so white. But they have community and direction, however delusional. I can't imagine what that would feel like—to have your purpose all figured out and a whole lifetime to get good at what you know you should be doing.

Camus takes my hand as we walk through Granada and tour the Alhambra. I watch him run his fingers along the Islamic carvings, dip his face into the vast flower gardens. He's short for his age and small boned, but his slight paunch and severe comb-over, the weary look in his eyes, and the way he shuffles along as though weighted down make him look like a tiny old man. He picks a few carnations for his parents, but very quickly puts them into a trash can. He picks me a red rose and asks, "Are you my brother?"

"No, Camus, you know we're not brothers."

"Are you my friend?"

"Yes, Camus, we're friends."

Later, after seeing fountains and tall trees, after watching young couples kiss beneath these trees, we walk up the narrow cobbled streets of the Moorish Quarter to the inhabited caves overlooking the city. It's dark and I hold Camus' hand tightly. He points toward the city lights below and says, "I can see our room from here."

"That's amazing," I say.

"And there's my mommy and daddy," he adds, pointing.

"There they are."

"They see me," he says. "Look, they're waving!"

"I can't see them, but I believe you."

"They're waving at me," he insists; then, "I think you're my best friend. Is that okay?"

"That's okay, Camus. We'll be best friends."

"My dad says all the writers are hacks, except for Sharini who he says is one gifted bitch. He says you're a lackey. What does it mean, Ted?"

"I don't know; I don't have any idea." I can see he's disappointed.

An old man comes out of a cave and Camus asks him questions about living in caves, but the man only smiles and touches Camus on the head.

"He doesn't speak English," I say.

"Is that why he lives in a cave?"

"No, he lives in a cave because he's poor."

"Oh," he says and gives the old man the stack of money his mom gave him, and the man touches Camus' head again, and laughs.

In the night, I'm awoken by Olivier, who, with something like shit on his breath, snarls, "That's right, sleep the sleep of the innocent while I grapple with true human suffering."

From Granada, we head to Morocco, "on the trail of Paul Bowles," as Dr. Doveman puts it. In Casablanca, Mrs. Doveman switches from Rioja to Stork beer, and Camus decides money is more fun to steal than lighters and matches. He divides his swindling fairly evenly between his parents and the other writers, and gives it all away to child beggars, who he believes live in caves. I could put a stop to it, but I respect his ability to act out, and I think that while his parents try to squash him into a mature literary figure, it's my job to let him go as far as he can in anything he genuinely feels like doing.

Under the absurd Moroccan sun, Dr. Doveman's sweating has reached new heights. He carries three, sometimes four shirts and makes a huge presentation changing into each one. Standing shirtless before us, eyes on Eli, he brags about his football days and unconsciously flexes—his tall, pale body thick with black hair and the memory of muscle. A twitching nipple: I think Eli is starting to notice.

Occupation #479: Sociologist.

The writers give a reading in a quiet café filled with international students. Everyone is moved by Sharini's poems and by the obvious animosity she holds for us all. She understands the world intuitively and looks down on those of us whom the world flusters. Though I am often confused by my world, her work makes perfect sense to me. She says the things I already knew, but could never have put into words. I want to tell her how much I respect her work, and I would if she weren't so mean and unapproachable and if it would interest her in the slightest, which it wouldn't, because clearly the au pair boy's opinion isn't worth snot.

Helene reads a confusing sestina about a battle between flapjacks and empathy, and Camus goes through her bag

looking for money. Dr. Doveman and Eli are talking in a
corner table, their faces too close, while Mrs. Doveman is at
the bar talking to what must be her sixth bottle of Stork.
Olivier sits alone, hair wild, with his old pen and lined
paper. He seems close to something big—to discovery, to
breakdown. Who can tell which? Most of the other people
in the bar have their eyes closed, intent on Helene's pan-
cake battle or perhaps their own momentous thoughts.
Camus catches my eye and smiles. He holds up his cash
booty and waves it around for everyone to see, which
nobody does.

In Fez, Michaelangelo announces that the Moroccans are
an uneducated and uncultured people. Eli says he'd do anything to shed himself of his education, which he claims
makes it impossible for him to "write anything of any degree
of competence, and why shouldn't I just slit my wrists, any-
how?" Beatrice says her dead boyfriend's dark, good looks
made him look Moroccan, and she breaks into tears.
Camus' thievery has likely led to a whole generation of
wealthy Moroccan beggar children. Olivier, unshaven
unbathed unhealthy, takes me aside and whispers, "I'm not
there yet, Ted, but listen closely: 'From sunshine comes
death, while moonshine brings breath.'" I nod and he goes
away. I doubt he's close to any sort of discovery, but I envy
the way he absolutely believes he is. Dr. Doveman likens
the Moroccan heat to the awesome and destructive passion

of Romeo for his Juliet. He drinks steaming cups of hot tea, sweats more than ever, and sways his pale and shirtless body to mating music I cannot hear.

It's strange how they all sleep with each other. And so loudly! They have sex like they write, with much drama, suffering, and noise. I believe this is the way writers bond. And also because they're all alcoholics. It started the first night, in Verona, when Eli had Helene. He had Beatrice on the following afternoon, and, later that night, gave Olivier the only blow job he'd ever received from a male. Then Olivier, confused for the first time about his sexuality, had Helene four times in a single afternoon. Sharini had Helene. Mrs. Doveman had Michaelangelo, and she continues to have Michaelangelo whenever she wants because he thinks she can help his career, which she can't. Olivier had Beatrice. Michaelangelo had Beatrice. Sharini had Eli. The Dovemans have nightly marathon sessions that culminate in Dr. Doveman screaming, "Don't you give up on me!" before howling minutes later. Most of them have no idea of what's going on, and imagine they've had a romantic and isolated European fling. They tell me everything. They have to tell someone and I'm not a person so much as a harmless au pair—a body in charge of keeping a smaller body out of their way.

People talk about living vicariously and all that garbage, but it isn't working for me. Mine is a penetration-free life:

it's just me and Camus for two more weeks, and then he'll go back with Dr. and Mrs. Doveman to their Berkeley home, ignored, reading books he can't understand, being told how far off he is from the person they want him to be.

On another train, during what will be an epic thirty-seven-hour train/ferry/train trip from Fez to Krakow (more specifically, from Fez to Tangier to Algeciras to Madrid to Paris to Prague to Krakow)—which Dr. Doveman says is meant to "echo the illusion of love's permanence in *Romeo and Juliet*"—the writers and Dr. Doveman try to hold a conversation using only lines from poetry and fiction.

Beatrice says, "'Look how peaceful these wooden figures are, going to their death.' Gerald Stern."

"'I find my clothes as barbarous as theirs,'" Eli says, "'only I don't butter my hair.' Arthur Rimbaud."

"'Good gentle youth,'" Dr. Doveman says, "'tempt not a desperate man.' *Romeo and Juliet*, act 5, scene 3." Dr. Doveman directs all his lines to Eli. If he merely had a crush on him before, it has clearly blossomed into full-blown love. Am I the only one who notices him pointing out chest moles and ingrown hairs to Eli as though seduction were a hideous thing? Though Mrs. Doveman is still sleeping with Michaelangelo (her bloated hand even now circling his knee), I have the feeling he has never cheated on her—that their marriage is a sort of barter: her endless devotion to his work in exchange for a young lover now and then, and his fidelity.

"Oh, tempt away," Helene counters, "for 'Naked, you are blue as a night in Cuba.' Pablo Neruda."

"And besides, 'Tis better to rule in Hell than to serve in Heaven.' Milton," Olivier says.

"And do you all know what the road to hell is paved in?" Dr. Doveman asks. "Who knows what the road to hell is paved in?"

"I know this," Eli says. "I know this."

"The road to hell is paved in . . . what?" Dr. Doveman repeats.

"Oh, man, how I know this!" Eli says.

"You've got it, son, don't give up!" Dr. Doveman urges.

None of the others knows, and since Eli will never get it, I say, "'Unbought stuffed dogs.' Ernest Hemingway."

"The au pair speaks," Sharini says.

"The au pair reads," Dr. Doveman says.

"I'm not an idiot," I say, suddenly and with too much vehemence.

"Of course you're not," Mrs. Doveman says. "You read a book. You remembered a line. Clearly, you're a genius." I keep my head down. She continues, "Now, *writers*, shall we continue this exercise?"

Occupations 82–84: Ditchdigger, Dogcatcher, Doorman.

"I am more foolish than the au pair," Eli says sadly, as though unable to conceive of a lousier fate.

"No," the others say.

"No, of course not," Dr. Doveman says. "Don't you believe that for a second."

So they continue, allowing Eli to begin with anything he'd like. "I can't think of a single line," he says.

"'Sad is the man who is asked for a story and cannot come up with one.' Li-Young Lee," Sharini says.

"Come on, Eli," Helene says, "'Say something about pomegranates. Say something about real love.' Yusef Komunyakaa."

"'Speak with the broken teeth of the squalid poop-chute of your soul,'" Michaelangelo quotes. "From my last unpublished novel."

"I've got one!" Eli is jubilant. "The only one: Kafka. 'What have I in common with Jews? I hardly have anything in common with myself, and should be happy to sit here, alone in a corner, content that I can breathe.'"

Then there's silence.

"Jesus," Helene says, "what a downer."

Mrs. Doveman leans toward me and hisses, "And where is Camus?"

"He's here," I say, gesturing to the empty seat beside me. And then I'm squatting under the empty seat and under all the seats. And now it's me and two Spanish guys in gray and brown uniforms, and we're searching back and forth across the train and they're calling out, "*Hijo! Hijo! Donde estas Camus?*" and each time we pass Mrs. Doveman she gives us a more condescending look and flares her nostrils in a way that makes all of us afraid, I think, and I can't believe I've lost him. I think about all the kids I've ever been in charge of—in boats, on hikes, building fires, leaping off high dives. How ridiculous it was that I never really worried about those once-a-summer William Tell incidents some brave/stupid kid would attempt—how I never felt anything was seriously at stake. I open the door to all the couchettes, exposing surprised faces, bored faces, sleeping faces. I can feel my heart.

Then one of the Spanish men calls out "*Gracias a Maria!*" and I rush over and Camus is asleep on a windowsill behind a drawn curtain. "Camus!" I say, and scoop him up. He's dusty, and there are window-frame prints on his cheek and ear, and when he sees my face he, too, breaks into tears. I haven't cried since I was a boy and the release is overwhelming.

"Camus," I say, "you scared the crap out of me." I hug him tightly, not sure why I'm so angry. "Don't you ever run away again!" I shake him, aware that I'm yelling, and aware that my yelling is only making him cry harder.

"I got lost," he says.

"No. You ran away." I hug him and he cries. I'm shaking.

Our second day in Krakow, Olivier refuses to come out of his dorm room, claiming, "All this traveling about is hindering the advance of my poetic truth." Mrs. Doveman sends Camus and me out to fetch him pierogi and juice.

From inside his room comes movie-villain laughter. Camus knocks and I call out, "Olivier, we've got your lunch here."

The room is littered with broken bottles, broken pencils, and about a million scraps of paper. *Die Fools!* is scrawled on a wall in, I suspect, blood, and what can only be human excrement has been thrown onto the wall across from it—the two declarations facing off like some ghastly joust of fluids versus solids. Cigarette smoke hovers like storm clouds, and Olivier, perched Indian style in the center of the bed, his quilted fez askew, looks dirty, happy, and very artsy.

"It smells in here," Camus says.

"My body is free from soap," Olivier announces, and awkwardly embraces me. He reaches for Camus, who hides behind my leg.

"How are those heroic couplets coming?" I ask.

"Let me tell you something, Ted. I used to think that my life and my genius would end up like *Romeo and Juliet*, act 5, scene 3, 'I am the greatest, able to do least.' But Ted, I'm almost there—and no, it's not about superiority and disgust for the masses as I once thought: It's about love and kindness and something about moonlight but I haven't figured that part out yet. I'm close, damn it, and I have the feeling that people will read these couplets forever. Can you imagine what that feels like? It's ecstasy, Ted. Ecstasy." Then he begins eating the pierogi, one after another, and it's as if we're not there anymore, so Camus pilfers a handful of change and we bolt.

Camus suggests we spend the day writing in a café as his father does. We walk around Krakow looking for just the right place, entering one after another, but Camus constantly complains: "No, Ted, this one is filled with hacks," or, "God, no, Ted, I said café, not coffee shop." Every once in a while he takes out a plain composition notebook, the same kind Dr. Doveman is constantly scribbling in, and scribbles something. He's obviously decided that the best way into his father's life is to mimic him as closely as he can. Still, he's just Camus and we laugh together about the cuteness of the Polish language—at the signs advertising *filmowi* and *hotelowi* and *hot-dogi*.

Eventually we find a literary-looking place near the Rynek Glowny and Camus pulls out two composition notebooks and orders us two cappuccinos. When our drinks come, Camus complains to me that his isn't strong enough, and that he can't tolerate a weak cappuccino. Then he scoops twenty-six spoonfuls of sugar into it. I ask him what we should write in our notebooks. He takes me by the forearm, a gesture Dr. Doveman is famous for, and says, "Whatever you write Ted, goddamnit, make sure it's honest."

"Yes, Camus, I'll try to be as honest as I can," I say, and then I write an actual poem, without rhyme and everything. I maybe copied a few things from Sharini, a bit of obliqueness from Helene, but the poem is mine. Is this all it takes to be a writer: space to work, a small amount of confidence, and caffeine?

Beside me, Camus plunges his head into his hands. "Goddamnit, Ted, I can't find my moose." He's drawn pictures of monkeys in trees under a frowning sun.

"Stop talking like your dad," I say. "Muse," I add.

"Without a visit from the moose, you're nothing but a hack, but, goddamnit, Ted, you still have to be honest."

"Stop. You're Camus. You're perfect just the way you are."

"You get money to say that," he says. "My mom pays you to be my friend."

"Oh, Camus." I pick him up and bring him onto my lap. "You and I are friends. We're buds." *All we have is each other*, I want to say. He looks away shyly, pinches my nose, and he's just a kid again with eyes seeming to say *Help me!*, but when the waitress walks by, those eyes harden and he calls out, "Mademoiselle, may we have two gin and tonics, easy on the tonic, if you know what I mean," which clearly neither of them do.

People have begun to notice their missing cash. Theories abound as to the culprit. Eli is convinced that Helene is taking the equivalent of two dollars for every night he doesn't sleep with her, so he begins sleeping with her. Michaelangelo believes the other writers are "trying to shake my unshakable confidence via a senseless campaign of thievery and deception." Beatrice, though she's drunk, confides in me that her dead boyfriend has returned from heaven to reclaim the two hundred dollars she owed him before he died. Olivier corners me against St. Adalbert's Church and declares that the dirty Poles and the dirty Moroccans and even, he believes, the dirty Spaniards are in cahoots to bankrupt him before "my benevolent discovery of poetic truth can illuminate this dark and desperate world." He pauses to make sure I comprehend the graveness of the situation. "Or maybe the dirty Gypsies," he whispers.

Our Krakow reading is held in a candlelit bar in the Jewish section of town where *Schindler's List* was filmed, and amidst so many stories of atrocity, the writers begin to embrace their latent Judaism. Dr. Doveman stands shiny faced on a makeshift stage reading from his new work-in-progress (Mrs. Doveman taking notes, taking vodka shots, taking photographs), while at our large, round table, Olivier, a yarmulke atop his head, broods over the international plot against him, and the other writers speak in coded mathematics, each trying to über-Jew the other. Helene says, "My uncle married a Jew, and when he divorced her, he married another Jew, which I think makes me one-twelfth Jewish."

"I'm one-eighth Jew on my mother's side, and a quarter Jewish on my father's side," Eli says. "Though emotionally my Judaism accounts for a third of my character, at least."

"My great-grandparents were killed at Treblinka," Sharini says.

"Really?" I say.

"Yes. Really."

"Maybe even as high as one-half," Eli is saying.

"I think the dirty Jews are in on it, too," Olivier whispers into my ear. "Tell no one."

It's all a little too much and Camus is counting money beside me and Dr. Doveman, onstage, is screaming his finale, nearly in tears though nobody else is, and I'm drinking kosher beer. Camus scurries onto my lap and whispers, "Eli and Sharini think you're stealing their money and they gave me this much money to watch you," and he holds up a ten-*zloty* note.

"You know I'm not stealing, Camus."

"I know," he says. "I told them it was me, but they laughed and Eli kissed me on the face, and here's his passport," and he holds up a passport.

"What are you going to do with that?" I ask.

"I don't know. What should I do?"

"You should put it back. You should talk to your parents and tell them what you've done. They'll listen to you if you tell them."

"No," he says. "They won't listen and I don't want to tell them."

"Eli will be very sad if anything happens to his passport."

"I've seen Eli kiss Dad like Mom kisses Dad," he says, as though justifying anything he's planning to do.

Occupation #594: Wrecker. A person who demolishes or dismantles, or one who salvages and clears away wreckage.

Prague would be beautiful were it not so deeply shrouded in Eli's appropriation of Kafka's misery. How to enjoy the Charles Bridge, for example, after having it described by Eli as "lengthy as my sorrow, impenetrable as my suffering, cold and hard as my heart"? I suppose, however, that there is a certain beauty to Eli's woe. It's so overblown, yet completely sincere, and I can see that he's looking to it to save him.

I had thought that writers would look to their work to find some saving grace, but it seems as though their work most often distracts them from seeing anything at all. Olivier is an exception, believing his work and the truth it uncovers will save him, but look at Dr. Doveman, with his clammy seduction and his belief that Eli's misery can some-how save him. Michaelangelo, it occurs to me, is looking for Mrs. Doveman's connections to the world of publishing, and therefore *fame*, to save him, and Mrs. Doveman is putting her hopes on Dr. Doveman's fame, and Camus' potential (and on alcohol to shroud the lack of both). Sharini has her talent, and her anger to keep away any who would think to rescue her, and Beatrice has the pain of her lover's death. It doesn't matter whether or not she can imagine his face or the heat of his body against hers; it's the pain that can save her now, which she can hold on to at night and which holds her in return. I suppose Helene has abstraction and sex to divert her. Camus holds my hand and tells me the things he's stolen because he hopes I can save him, which is probably impossible, but is nonetheless the only way I can save myself.

Tonight, our writers read in an old, ornate auditorium with members of another writers' colony from Charles University who seem to suffer from the same range of prob-lems as we do. They have their lost loves, past abuses, chem-ical depressions, impending failures, sexual misadventures, and one Bosnian writer breaks down and cries while reading about a dead lover he can't get over, which makes Beatrice break down for her dead lover she can't get over, and so they all cry—all that pain bouncing around the old building, and even I start to tear up, though for reasons that have nothing to do with Beatrice or any of them. Camus closes his eyes and plugs his ears.

After everyone has had a good cry, Dr. Doveman makes his suggestion about wet clothes and dry martinis, and Camus insists we go along. In the smoky bar, I watch Camus try to engage his father in conversation. I watch him hop on one leg to divert Dr. Doveman's attention from Eli. I see the actual moment of resignation, the sinking of his little head, the emptying of his father's wallet.

And the writers . . . how to describe the debauchery? Like ass-sniffing dogs, the writers in our group hook up with the Prague writers, swapping self-pity for saliva and later, I suppose, semen. I see Olivier explaining the imminence of his discovery to a Slavic blond with a lame foot—the fascinated gape of foreplay on her face. I hear Helene moan and be moaned at. I look around for a nice au pair girl and maybe a kid for Camus, but there is none.

Later, walking through the dorm halls, the screams and groans of so much unleashed sex echo in a terribly arousing way.

The next morning, when we're supposed to be enjoying hard rolls and jam and getting on a train to Turkey, we all crowd in front of Beatrice's room without hard rolls and jam and try to convince her not to stay in Prague with Stjepan, the Bosnian writer with the dead lover who she insists is the carrier of her dead boyfriend's soul.

"Stjepan understands me better than I understand myself. He's my Romeo. I have dreamed of him!"

"Yes, dreams . . ." Dr. Doveman says, ". . . act 1, scene 4, 'dreams, which are the children of an idle brain, begot of nothing but vain fantasy: which is as thin of substance as the air and more inconstant than the wind.' *Romeo and Juliet*."

"But he's dreamed of me," Beatrice says.

"And so have I dreamed about you—and so has Mrs. Doveman dreamed about you—in Istanbul, dear. I have envisioned you in front of the Blue Mosque writing words as honest and delicious as milk chocolate."

"Come with us, dear," Mrs. Doveman says. "You need this trip, and we need you. Olivier needs you, and Michaelangelo, and this . . . ," and she points at me and frowns.

"Thief," someone says.

". . . and, well, certainly Eli needs you," she continues.

"Beatrice," Eli says, bored, "come on." Dr. Doveman squeezes his shoulder, says, "It's okay, son." Helene puts her hands in a prayer position: "act 1, scene 4," she says. "'You are a lover; borrow Cupid's wings, and soar with them above common bound.'" She kisses Beatrice on the forehead. Sharini scowls.

Dr. Doveman says, "act 2, scene 3, 'wisely and slowly; they stumble that run fast.'"

Beatrice says, "'Did my heart love till now? foreswear it sight! For I never saw true beauty till this night.' I don't know the act or the scene. I think it was in the beginning though."

Michaelangelo says, "'Young men's love, then lies, not truly in their hearts, but in their eyes.'"

"Indeed," Dr. Doveman says, "act 2, scene 3, if I'm not mistaken. My jiminy, if that's not insightful."

"We love each other a lot and fuck you all!" Beatrice says, and slams her door, and we stand there, hungry, listening to the pitter-patter of her weeping and the deep and sexy notes of Bosnian compassion.

Dr. Doveman says, "Act 2, scene 6, people: 'These violent delights have violent ends.' Nonetheless, Beatrice has made her foolish decision. We, however, are expected in Istanbul by one hundred or so of the most belletristic Turks you'd ever want to meet. Whom we will, meet that is, tonight, if we zip, which we will, right over to collect our pastries and jellies—we have a train to catch."

The others head back to their rooms and Camus appears beside me.

"Booty," he says, holding up money and passports.

"Booty," I say, poking him in his puny butt.

"Don't." I pick him up anyway, and he laughs and spanks me on the head with a stolen passport.

It's hard to say exactly where we are when the police come into our sleeping car to check our passports. It's me, Camus,

Helene, Michaelangelo. The police look disco-ish in tan pants and orange jackets. I find Camus' passport and mine no problem but feel a little sorry for Helene and Michaelangelo: emptying pockets and backpacks, sifting and then resifting, disbelieving.

"It has to be here!" Helene says.

"I never lose anything!" Michaelangelo says.

"Here's ours," I say.

And then we're milling about the narrow train corridor with the other writers and Mrs. Doveman. Dr. Doveman is talking with the police behind the closed door of his couchette, and Camus sleeps soundly in my arms. Me, the au pair, the only one who knows exactly what's happened.

"Nobody panic," Mrs. Doveman says, drinking from a silver flask, "Dr. Doveman was called 'America's only living genius' by the *Salt Lake City Tribune*. He'll get us out of this."

"Somebody is going to get shot here," Sharini says, looking at me.

The policemen and Dr. Doveman come out of the couchette all smiles. "Change of plans," Dr. Doveman says. "We won't be going to Istanbul."

"No Turkey?" Eli says, sadly.

Dr. Doveman embraces Eli in a bear hug: "Yes, my boy, certainly Turkey. Marmaris, Turkey. We'll disembark at the next stop, escorted by these four enterprising magistrates, where we'll travel to Bucharest, and from Bucharest to Edirne, Turkey, where these gentlemen assure me we can enter with some rather expensive visas they've sold me. From there, we'll travel by bus to Marmaris, charter a boat, and let things cool down while we figure out a way to complete the Veronese Circle *sans* passports." He gives us two thumbs up, smiling broadly as though he does this sort of thing all the time.

Thirty-six hours later, Dr. Doveman says, "We're about chin deep in a very large heap of shit." We're on a yacht-like boat, on lounge chairs drinking cold Turkish beer in the hot Mediterranean sun, and I can't imagine feeling less like I was in a heap of shit. Our illegal bus ride through Romania and across the border was one for the books. I have never felt so clearly and unabashedly criminal, and so completely not myself. I kept thinking about Occupation #345: Product Namer. I felt that same sense of possibility during the clandestine bus trip that I imagine product namers must feel gazing upon an unnamed product. "There's a thief among us," Dr. Doveman continues, "and until this numbnuts returns our passports, we aren't going anywhere." He looks each of us in the eye. "Ted," he says, "you haven't had your passport stolen, have you?"

"No," I say.

"Interesting," he muses, "that you're the only one, besides Camus, which could constitute a clue, if this were a crime of sorts, which it is."

"Oh, just give it the fuck up, Ted," Michaelangelo says.

"Let's slit open his belly," Sharini suggests.

"Act 3, scene 2," Mrs. Doveman says, completely smashed, "'There's no trust, no faith, no honesty in men.'"

I look around at them, at all the eyes suddenly on me (a not unpleasant feeling) and it's as if all the dramatic language I've had pounded into my head by them suddenly arranges itself into an order that makes sense, and I realize I've finally been invited to take part in their drama. I say, "I haven't taken anything from any of you, except your insults and your condescension, and now your suspicion. You probably threw away your passports in some unconscious act of self-sabotage, and I can't wait to hear the volumes of rueful literature you'll produce about your wretched imprisonment on a Turkish boat. You want thieves? You're the thieves! Search me. Search my valise and search up my ass if it'll ease your fragile souls. I'm as innocent as Camus!"

And I storm off, because storming off seems like the most appropriate option. And how great do I feel! *Valise?* Whose hat did I pull that beauty out of! I feel tragic and accused. Sitting alone on my narrow cot in the hot windowless berth, I realize they're no better or worse than I am. I can wear suffering just as smartly as they do.

So we float. We eat and drink, they write, there's a bit of waterskiing, and we wait for something to happen. For a thief to come forward. For passports to fall out of cloudless skies.

On the second night of this, I'm reading and Camus is lying on his cot covered by a pillow. My book says that, though finding an occupation is essential, "no book is going to solve your problem if you have one." It suggests getting out there and "experiencing the world of work and commerce."

I reread the three most difficult-sounding jobs, and wonder whether I'd have the balls to pursue one: Lifeguard, Justice of the Peace, Human Resources. Talk about daunting job titles! Talk about every day butting heads with your own limitations.

There's a single knock on our door. It's Olivier, clean shaven, slick hair, scent of baby powder.

"I am a genius," he announces, holding up a sheet of paper.

"Congratulations, Olivier," I say. "You've finished."

"Yes, yes," he says. "We all knew I could do it. Allow me to read you the central tercet of the piece. If you listen carefully, Ted, you'll likely perceive a poetic truth." He clears his throat.

"'Kiss the moon. Beam. Forge / the alliance. The heart, salmon, / unclad, Love's acrimonious appliance.'"

How to respond?

"It's wonderful, Olivier! Pregnant with poignance!"

"Yes, thank you. I meant salmon colored, you know."

"Oh!"

"Not the fish, of course."

"Wow, I'm really impressed, Olivier. It's genius."

He takes my hand in both of his and says, "Thank you, Ted. Thank you. And nice speech the other day." He walks out.

"What a hack," Camus says from beneath his pillow. His stumpy legs jut out from beneath the pillow in tiny tweed pants, but otherwise he's entirely protected.

Who's to say? Maybe there was a poetic truth in there, and you just needed to be Olivier to find it. "He works as well as he can, Camus. At least he's trying. At least he's failing."

It's enough already. The air feels so ripe with impotence—is positively begging for action. "Camus," I say, "I'm going to tell your parents that you're the one with the passports."

He doesn't move.

"No," he finally says, his voice muffled by pillow. "You can't tell on me. You're my best friend."

"And you're my best friend, Camus, but we can't just do nothing. How can we fix anything by doing nothing?" I remove the pillow, muss up his waxy comb-over, kiss his forehead. "I'm sorry," I say, and stride purposefully out of our berth. I stop for a bit on the main deck and consider the meteor shower in the night sky. All those old stars hurtling themselves to death in some celestial last hurrah. "You're killing yourself," I'd warn, if stars could understand—if they would let themselves be helped. I think about Romeo and Juliet and what an ugly thing fate is—how violently we battle against it. I can't save Camus any more than I can save that star there . . . or that one. In ten years he'll be pretentious, enraged, and self-loathing. He will be utterly unlikable.

At the Dovemans' berth, Mrs. Doveman, ripe with brandy, answers in a thin white robe. "Dr. Doveman is disappeared," she says. "I cannot find him anywhere."

"It's Camus," I say. "Camus is the thief."

"What are you saying?" she screams dramatically, as though this were community theater.

Then Camus is beside me and I make a gesture meant to say *Aha! The thief in the flesh*, but the way Camus is tugging on the bottom of my shirt tells me that something is very wrong. He pulls me back toward our berth, a brandy-pickled Mrs. Doveman scantily arranged and in tow.

The door is hot, and when I fling it open, I see that two walls and both our cots are engulfed by flames.

I say, "Camus, what happened?"

"I don't know," he says. He's still holding on to my shirt, there are tears, and I imagine him burning money and passports—the easy way things can get out of control. "Put it out, Ted," he says.

So I try. And when I fail, the captain tries, and soon all of us are standing on the main deck buttoning up life jackets. "We're missing Dr. Doveman and Eli!" someone screams.

"I will rescue them!" Michaelangelo yells, but doesn't move. The heat from the flames is enormous.

I take Camus by the hand and jump overboard. We land together, side by side, the water calm and refreshing as a lukewarm bath. Soon Helene and Michaelangelo splash nearby, and then Sharini. Olivier calls out, "'I must be gone and live, or stay and die!'" and then casts himself among us. Mrs. Doveman belly flops, and the captain executes a perfect swan dive deep into the phosphorescent sea. He emerges about thirty yards from us and swims quickly and efficiently toward the distant shore. He yells something to us in Turkish that sounds vaguely hopeful. Eventually, Eli and Dr. Doveman appear glistening at the flaming edge of the ship, buck naked save for their life jackets, their erections like arrows indicating the location of the polestar. Hand in hand they jump.

Nobody speaks and we float in the warm sea, watching shooting stars and burning ship. Camus, snuggling against my hip and stomach, swirls his hands through the water.

"Look at the lights," he says, of the phosphorescent bubbles following the trail of his little hands.

"Look at the lights," I say, pointing to the sky.

"Beautiful, right?" he says, speaking of one or maybe the other.

We won't make it to Verona again to complete the circle of our trip. We won't be there to wish on the time- and wear-faded bronze breast of Juliet and remember how it feels to know you can't have what you most want.

"Oh Camus," I say, and place my arm over his shoulder to keep him from floating away.

DOCUMENTARY

THE SALT OF blood, hot sweat, the wide open vagina: These were the smells of childbirth, the camera implied. Instead, the truth was a pleasant, inhuman smell like wet pine wrapped in motel sheets, like a green apple lying on the ocean floor. Which was alarming, Samantha thought, that after just three days of filming, her documentary was already on the verge of inaccuracy. She'd considered a voiceover pointing out the discrepancy between sight and smell, but wasn't sure anybody would believe that the violence they were watching had much to do with an old apple in the sea. In this, Samantha's first paid project (she'd won a grant from the Maternity Center Association), she'd come to see how many ways the medium of film reduced childbirth into contorted faces, ridiculous patterns of breathing, fitness-room words of encouragement (*Come on now! One more time and . . . push!*), and all the fluids the body could make at once.

She had no background in medicine and wasn't exactly sure why she'd written out the grant proposal. She'd simply felt surrounded by babies; her younger sister had just given birth to her second, and most of her friends were either pregnant or had pink newborns. It seemed every adult pushed a stroller or wore some elaborate child-harness, and so she'd begun to read the *New England Journal of Medicine* and *Parenting* magazine—and between the Learning Channel and the Health Channel she was watching six hours of births a week. These were medical shows, though, showing statistics and facts without too much reflection. Her film would take the facts and use them to make discoveries.

She was looking for something like a truth, something she and her film could be said to have discovered. Something specific, like the better the conception-sex the healthier the child, or maybe she'd find that babies born at night were less prone to needing night-lights. Was the process of giving birth traumatic enough to actually age a woman, and if so, what was the numerical correlation: one hour of labor for each month of aging?

She wasn't so sure what she was looking for.

She knew, however, that her truth would reveal itself through the images of birth, and the image that continually drew her in was the moment of release, when the baby ceased being part of its mother, along with the blood, plasma, umbilical cord, membranes, water, urine—the unbelievable amount of gunk that fairly gushed from between a new mother's legs. This was the point of transition from fetus to human being, and from woman to mother. She'd experimented with this moment, splicing together all the births she'd filmed so far into one large eruption, surprised at the seamlessness of switching from one vagina to another—how similar it all looked and how easily the images could be weaved together to create one endless fountain of birth. She'd tried something similar in grad school, patching together the male orgasms from a few pornographic films to create one mondo shoot-off, cups of it supposed to have been launched from the same large phallus. The angles, of course, were all wrong; it was obvious when one penis became another. Here, though, it seemed birth was birth—that in trying to record the unfolding of life, all she'd succeeded in capturing were vaginas: stretched, generic vaginas expelling screaming, generic babies.

Josef called that last instant "womb soup." He called it the eruption of Mount Vaginas. They sat in front of the twenty-dollar used television in their Brooklyn apartment drinking whiskey with buttermilk because Josef had somehow confused it with eggnog, and they watched today's five births. It was Christmas Eve, and a few haphazardly wrapped presents lay scattered under a poinsettia on the kitchen table. They sipped their awful drinks, watched the children being born, and Josef hugged his knees and called it disgusting.

"It's not disgusting!" she said. "Quit being such a puss."

"No, Sam, it is, it's totally disgusting."

"It's beautiful," she said. "Why can't you see that?"

Josef made large, brightly colored paintings of animals having sex with people, of animals having sex with other animals while people watched, of people having sex with animals while other animals watched. Six months ago, he'd painted a ferret having sex with his stepfather while his mother watched. He'd sent it to them for their tenth anniversary. Recently, these paintings had begun to sell in the Chelsea gallery where they hung; last week, Josef and the gallery owner agreed to double the prices, a move which seemed to improve sales.

He hadn't always painted such pictures; when they'd moved in together, Josef was working on a series of dark, spare landscapes. They were just cityscapes and rural villages—land and sky—but in their depiction he'd managed to attach the sorrows of the people who invisibly inhabited them. Every time she looked at one she wanted to cry. He'd tapped into something with these paintings; they were more powerful than they should have been. He'd come home from his studio drained but excited, and Sam would allow him to brag a bit because she was proud as well. For the past fourteen months, however, long enough that Sam was beginning to doubt it would ever end, it was just the animals, the people, and the sex. She could remember the first time she'd seen one of these pictures, the same disconcerting jolt as when she'd seen the way Josef's name was spelled. She'd thought of him as plain old "Joseph," but suddenly he was

Slavic. Both events made her think, *Who is this guy?* The sex paintings hung on most walls of their apartment, and sometimes—fornicating animals staring at her from all sides—she'd wonder about the set of decisions which had led her to call this place home.

"Look," he said, "you know I love kids, but this . . ." and he pointed to the doctor performing an episiotomy on the television. "I mean, her cervix is heaving. It's goddamned heaving!"

She tried not to laugh. He often made her laugh at the same time he made her angry. The problem with Josef, she thought, was that he was so uncomfortable with uncertainty that he resisted everything new. It had taken him two years to tell her he loved her, and even then he seemed to say it not to her directly but to the painting beside her head (his painting: fish sprouts dick, nun on knees sucks the dick, family of bears watch with opera glasses), so that she wasn't convinced he loved her and not just his work. He'd improved over the past year, and now when he told her he loved her, he said it to her foot, or sometimes her ear. He was thirty-two, she was thirty-three.

"Here," she said, taking his hand. "Come with me."

She led him into their bedroom, where she'd hung "Rules for Living." She picked up a pen, thought a moment, and wrote, "There is nothing so simple about childbirth that it can be summed up in one word, especially if that word is 'disgusting.'" She numbered this rule #3—the list was only a month old. Rule #2 said, "Celebrate everything." Yes, he was expected to attend her MFA graduation, and no, his presence there wasn't celebration enough. She'd accomplished something and you acknowledged this just as you acknowledged a three-year anniversary with more than a card, as Josef had almost done. (It was this, finally, which prompted writing #2.) You set time aside so the two of you could put to words what three years had meant, because if you didn't, you could forget to see; you could miss significance if you never found the right words to name it. It could get to where nothing had any weight, where love was merely a penis placed into a vagina, and bucking hips.

That night, they opened their Christmas presents. They'd agreed not to buy each other too much, yet he surprised her with an enormous bouquet of flowers, a handmade silk dress she'd lingered over in a boutique a few months before, and what she thought was the most beautiful bracelet she'd ever seen: a perfect circle of amethyst, her birthstone, traced with white gold. She loved her gifts but they made her anxious. This was the time to save for adult things like cars with baby seats, or an apartment and new furniture to fill the apartment. She got him pants and shirts, a belt and socks, all from a chain store that catered to young professionals. Josef had the unfortunate habit of buying clothes at thrift shops, thinking they were trendy and alternative, but really the collars were just too big and they smelled sour and withered.

After the presents, they brushed the film of buttermilk from their teeth, and slept.

Sam had been given ten days to film at Beth Israel Medical Center in the East Village. Mornings were spent meeting new couples, getting signed releases—there were often long periods of nothing to do except stare at Christmas decorations and Hanukkah cards until, usually all at once, each new room she entered held masked doctors and a frightened man crouched over an open-legged woman. And then she'd crouch beside the woman as well, recording the awkwardness and anger that accompanied birth, the spontaneous blessings when women turned away from pain and spoke to their future children: *This is how you came into the world, angel*, or, *I do this out of love for you, my child.* One mother yelled out, *You'll pay for this!*

Birth wasn't always the monument to love that television preached; there were often bitter arguments between husband and wife, and wife and doctor—well, mostly just the wife yelled and the doctors and husbands took it. One woman, a high-pitched, small-boned pastry chef, punched her husband in the head, pulled out clumps of his hair, and finally scratched the mask off his face, before realizing—and it was a moment Sam had recognized in other mothers—that her pain was far greater than any she could inflict with punches or scratches, and so she resorted to a more powerful weapon: words. "You loser!" she screamed.

"You monkey! You prick . . ." Then, with a snarl, she spat out, "Hate you!" and he backed against a wall, bloodied and terrified. "Get it out of me!" she screamed. "Get this thing the fuck out of me!" And they did. The doctor got the baby out, placed it gray and creamy onto her chest (her husband hesitantly making his way back to her), and just ten minutes later she asked Sam, "Did you get it? Did you capture the miracle of my baby's birth?"

In the hours and days following delivery, the parents she'd filmed became increasingly dependent upon her. They needed her, she came to realize, because she was their witness. The women needed confirmation that their pain had been like a physical presence bearing down on them with all the force it could summon and changing them in the process, because it wasn't just the baby that was a miracle. And it was easy for Sam to confirm this, because she'd never seen anything like it. These women, almost always younger than she, seemed positively alien; opened up by pain, their screams like the singing of an exotic creature.

Was it even possible, she wondered, that somewhere within her lay that same song?

The fathers needed Sam in a different way. They were afraid of her because she had seen them scared and helpless. The men wanted to hear that they had been a different person in the delivery room—that their cowardice was something separate from their real selves. What they really wanted, Sam thought, was to be told they were no longer just men, but fathers; that they would never again feel as help-less as they had in the delivery room because back then they had just been men.

Nothing, however, was said out loud. The new parents pleaded silently, bribed her with offers of hospital tea, held out their babies for one last touch; the camera, of course, only captured the obvious—the pastry chef thrashing her husband, then, the two of them lovingly cradling their new child—and without any words of explanation, you could miss the transition. Yet, sometimes, watching over her footage, she'd catch a glimpse of the metamorphosis as it occurred, so that one could see both the caterpillar and the butterfly, or in this case, both the woman and mother, man and father. *There*! she'd shout to the crappy, fuzzy television screen, but it was already gone.

It was fitting, Sam thought, that after a day of recording births, she'd come home to an apartment whose walls cele-brated sex (however bright and unlikely). She'd begun to see the unconscious connection between their projects— Josef's sex and her birth: an elaborate dialogue between cause and effect. They'd started out as simple amusement— a break from the intensity of the landscapes—and when they'd first begun to sell, he was angry, having not yet sold a single landscape. He and Sam would curse the art world's awful taste, and it was fun to be united with him against everyone else. Eventually, as the paintings continued to sell,

Josef grew less angry. Samantha, however, hated seeing his signature on them, and she missed the landscapes as though they were a friend who'd simply disappeared.

On her fifth day of filming, Sam thought she saw a baby die. It emerged from within its mother vacant-eyed, unflopping, unscreaming. *This*, she thought, *this is the way these things happen—quietly, in sterile rooms surrounded by people trained to stop it.* But then one of the doctors, a tall, wide-shouldered man, did stop it—tapped the baby casually on the back as though saying, "Live, why don't you?" which it did, sputtering and wheezing and crying the particular animal cry of the recently born.

The doctor made nothing of it, claimed the baby's breathing was "simply obstructed." He was lying, though; Sam knew he was. That baby was dead, and the doctor's tap, like an inserted key, turned it back on. It was one of the things that interested her most about childbirth: the way it perfectly bridged the gap between medicine and miracle. Precision could only get a doctor so far; being exceptional required an ability to see beyond the symptoms and the formulas—required, for instance, an intuitive impulse to tap a dying baby back to life.

That night, she met Josef at a gallery opening in Chelsea. The artist, a longtime supporter of Josef's work, sculpted enormous steel blobs. Josef had many such supporters because one of his rules for living was to never criticize another artist's work. Just praise, praise, praise. It was one of the things Sam liked least about him.

There were the usual beautiful people dressed in purposely ripped clothes and too-large sunglasses; waiters passed by with glasses of rosé because the artist was said to adore the color. Sam spotted Josef right away, laughing with two girls who shouldn't have been old enough to drink wine, even pink wine. She joined their group and the girls fled.

"Were they somebody's little sisters?"

"This is their gallery," he whispered.

"They look twelve," she whispered back, then, louder, "Why are you whispering?"

"Just keep it down, that's all."

"I saw a baby die today," she whispered, and it sounded real when spoken aloud.

"What's that?" he said.

"Forget it."

"Guess what?" he said. "My gallery sold a painting to an Italian count for four thousand dollars."

"Which one?"

"The coliseum orgy one with the football players and the polar bears."

"And the penguins watching, right?" A waiter passed by and she took a glass of wine.

He said, "It's gonna hang in a castle!"

Sam had grown up around artists (her father was a painter, her mother made animal figurines out of poppy seeds and bottle caps), had gone to grad school with other artists. Art was supposed to cost money! You weren't supposed to earn a living from it, *especially* if that art featured polar bears raping football players with goalposts.

"It's something," she said. The wine was awful. She hated these events. There was a time—she wasn't sure when it had ended—when she could have whispered how much she hated this place to Josef, and he would have mouthed the words *I hate it more.*

"I'm supposed to bring in the pictures from our apartment. The gallery is almost totally out of what I gave them."

"The ones on our walls?"

"We can't afford them anymore," he said, laughing.

"Who cares about the money?" she said, knowing that three months ago, four thousand dollars would have been like winning the lottery. Now though, she felt as if the color of her eyes was being taken away. "It's like you're selling off pieces of our home," she added.

"They have nothing to do with *our home.* I painted them hoping someone would pay me to put them in *their home.*"

"Our walls will be blank," she said, not knowing what else to say; her eyes were blue and she knew they were the first thing people thought pretty about her—brown-eyed, who would she be?

"I'll put the landscapes back up. Besides, you don't even like them."

"I never said that."

"You think I'm not aware of anything."

"I don't think that," she objected, though she wasn't sure whether she did or didn't.

"There's someone I have to talk to," he said, and disappeared into the crowd.

She helped herself to cheese cubes and cherry tomatoes. Everyone looked too young to be drinking. The sculpture in front of her was a blob stacked on top of another blob. A couple next to her gazed deeply at it and nodded knowingly. "Profoundly sexual," the woman said. The man winked and they rubbed noses.

She and Josef used to have a lot of sex. *The best sex ever*, she'd once told a friend. She wouldn't even believe it if the friend didn't still ask how all that amazing sex was coming along. Josef didn't like to massage her legs anymore, and complained that she wanted to talk for too long before sex and cuddle for too long after. The biggest problem, however, was the difficulty of mixing her anger and disappointment with the tenderness of lovemaking—to caress him and have him inside her. She could still hear the words: *I saw a baby die today.* She wondered how people learned to forgive.

It was only December 29, but the staff at Beth Israel had long been speculating about which of their pregnant mothers could possibly give birth to the first New York City baby of the year. All of the city's hospitals took part in this informal contest, though as far as Sam could tell, the only real prize was local news coverage and a certain amount of bragging rights at medical conferences. For the past three years, Mount Sinai Hospital had won, last year recording the birth of an eight-pound girl at 12:02 AM. Naturally, the Beth Israel nurses made it clear they'd never do anything to either postpone or rush a birth in order to coincide with the dropping of the Times Square ball, and the doctors refused to even admit such a competition existed (though she did notice a certain glint of hope when they discussed mothers who could possibly give birth on January 1).

As for the parents, they spoke openly about their desire to be first. When pressed, they couldn't define exactly what they hoped such an honor would lead to, and Sam could tell they wanted to win with the not-so-thought-out belief that it would give their child an advantage: to start out as a winner—featured on the news!—would provide a framework for things to come. It was like getting into the best preschool and then the best elementary, and while it seemed a ludicrous and futile hope, she understood that it was done out of utter terror—because they didn't know how to fully protect the life of their child, they reached blindly for anything which could somehow offer an advantage.

There was so much to believe in and so many things to fear (*I feel like there could be a monster inside me, like a lizard baby or something. Is that weird?*). Some mothers were sure their child would be born with thirteen toes, or no arms, or that when it stopped kicking for a minute it must have died; if they gave in to pregnancy cravings, their baby would be born without willpower, and if they named it John after their husband's father, the baby wouldn't be anything like *that* John, but would be like John Winterson from junior high, with his harelip and the rumors of a four-foot tapeworm. Rings swung in front of pregnant bellies to predict the baby's sex, the astrological consideration of due dates, and yes, that glass of wine they'd had in their second trimester would certainly lead to fetal alcohol syndrome. How simple it was to give in to fear when the words of a relative stranger controlled everything—*It's a boy*, or, *It's dead*—when the line between life and death was a careless tap on the back and nothing more.

She thought about love like that, blundering and eruptive; it must feel as though absolutely everything were at stake. She envied these women their vulnerability, thinking that in her own list of "Rules for Living," the first rule would say, "Be unafraid." Yet she was afraid—of her film, of Josef, of the doctors and their strange intuitions, and most of all of the babies, so tiny and barely human (fetuses just moments before), their deformed heads like alien heads, their cries like the drone of swarming insects.

Brunch. All of a sudden, Josef had opinions about brunch and the best places to get brunch. He even started using the word as a verb: *Should we brunch today?* In the past, he'd been perfectly happy with Apple Jacks and a banana, but now he talked about the complexities of hollandaise sauce and crêpes, all the things which could go wrong in the making of them—the dread of sour hollandaise or bulky crêpes.

This was apparently *the place* for brunch near Central Park. The opulence of the restaurant wasn't as shocking as the fact that Josef knew so many of the people there. He patted shoulders and shook hands the whole way to their table. "Artists and dealers," he explained. Josef ordered two bottles of what he called "a sick chardonnay," one for them and one for some gallery owners sitting at a corner table. He pulled out her chair for her, and when she sat down, he kissed her on the forehead. He was obviously proud to be able to take her here, and he looked like a little boy in his Christmas pants and shirt.

"You have to try their salmon Benedict," he said. "The hollandaise is beautiful. I'm getting lamb shank and eggs, but that's so we can share. And foie gras. We'll have that first." He closed his menu, folded his hands, and grinned. It was strange, the things that made him excited.

"You're very cute today," she said.

When the wine came, Josef ignored the offered splash in his glass, just bit the cork, nodded, and told the waiter to go ahead and pour. He had all sorts of bits he'd do with waiters and telemarketers.

Over hazelnut- and date-stuffed foie gras, Josef said, "I've been thinking about a new series of paintings: monkeys having sex with babies while really happy adults watch."

"That doesn't sound new," she said. The foie gras was about the best-tasting thing she'd ever eaten. She cut it into tiny pieces and didn't so much chew as just place it on her tongue until it dissolved.

"It is, though. It would just be the monkeys, maybe some orangutans, and they'd always be having sex with babies, and it would always be absurdly happy adults watching. It's about voyeurism and the reality TV phenomenon."

"I don't know. It might not be a good idea to make art about television."

"Oh, okay, hmm . . . then what should I paint? Since you seem to know."

"I'm not trying to tell you what to do, I'm only . . ."

"I mean, I must know something, right?" and he gestured across the restaurant and even toward the food on their plates as though the proof of his knowledge lay within the foie gras, along with the dates and the hazelnuts.

"Just because you're selling paintings doesn't mean . . ."

"Why can't you ever just be proud . . ."

". . . I think you're a great painter, but it's hard for me to be proud . . ."

". . . when I'm doing so well, and people are starting to pay attention to my work . . ."

". . . monkeys raping babies," she said.

". . . and not to yours," he said. "And it's not rape."

"I'm not jealous of you selling out," she said, and it felt good to say it. "I'm angry that people are buying *these* paintings and ignoring the landscapes, which were brilliant."

Josef laughed. "Brilliant, huh?"

"Yes, brilliant."

He reached across the table and took her hand, saying, "See, was that so hard?"

It was! Being kind was like admitting she was wrong, and she wasn't wrong. Sure, his new series had monkeys, babies, and sex, so it would be a huge hit, but it would also have about as much significance as discovering the perfect brunch; it wouldn't help anyone to figure out anything about the world.

Then again, it was just so much easier to hold his hand. And the wine seemed to change with each passing moment, growing richer and more complex, the flavors shifting from apples, to vanilla, to honey, to something like caramelized pears. Maybe she *should* just be proud of him.

When their entrées came, Josef picked up his lamb shank by the bone and told it to take it like a man. She tried to swallow her laugh with a bite of salmon, which was buttery, unusual, and delicious.

Later, they found a bench in the park and watched families walk by. It seemed everyone was traveling in families today, strollers and double strollers, children clinging to shoulders—and twins, everyone had a set, and triplets, and what was it called when you had four at once? Sam herself had two sisters and a brother and had always wanted four kids of her own, but even if it were possible at her age to have a baby a year for four years, what would it be like: A thirty-seven-year-old documentary filmmaker coming home to four crying babies gathered around a husband painting four crying babies being sodomized by a family of monkeys?

She could have four at once, she supposed, like that couple there—though they had the too-much-torture look of returning MIAs. She didn't want to be one of those worn, desperate women on fertility drugs. So far she'd filmed six sets of twins being born, the eerie quiet that fell between one birth and the other. They were always so creepy, twins, with their matching outfits, speaking languages only the other one understood. Sam remembered the hours spent in front of mirrors when she was a young girl, watching herself dance to see how her body moved, experimenting with different smiles—trying on gestures and expressions like costumes—wanting to figure out what she was. How then . . . this generation of twins born to parents too old to have children . . . how will they figure out anything when everywhere they look they see another self acting in unfamiliar and undesirable ways?

She found herself thinking about that baby that had almost died, and wishing that it had, and even wishing there had been two dead babies, twins. Stories needed clear, direct tragedy, not the read-between-the-lines kind her film was exposing. Yet where had such a thought come from? Wishing for dead babies wasn't who she was unless she'd changed into someone else. Beside her, Josef wore that detached look he got when he drank and Sam considered how far away motherhood seemed—how each year it just grew more and more distant.

"All these fucking twins," she said.

"It's the puppet show," Josef said.

"No, it's the fertility drugs these old fucks have to take."

"No, I mean the puppet show," and he pointed, and yes, there was a puppet show going on, and it was here that all the parents and their children gathered.

"I don't want twins," she said.

In the hospital yesterday, a woman had stood up in the middle of labor and announced she was leaving. *That's it*, she had said, *I'm not having this baby*, and she walked maybe three steps. The doctor let her go to show she had no choice now. She'd have the baby whether she liked it or not. Family was like that, Sam thought, and thank God it was. She loved her big, loud family, but loved even more the permanence of it—the way they'd always be her family no matter how much they pissed each other off.

"Okay," he said, "you won't have twins. I didn't even realize you were having kids. Are you having them without me?"

"If I have to."

"What does that mean?"

"It means I want to have kids . . ."

"But not twins."

"It means I don't want to wait until I'm so old I'll need drugs, which will give me twins. That's what it means."

"Well," he said, "someday," and took her hand in his own, which was moist and alternated between squeezing too hard and not squeezing hard enough. She held on anyway. She didn't need four children. Even two seemed too much to hope for. *Thirty-three*, she thought. *Thirty-three*. And though she knew it might just be the wine reacting with the hollandaise, right then Samantha could very clearly feel her own transition—from childbearing age to *just too old*. The delicate ache of her eggs rotting.

"No hurry," she said. "In two years my chances of giving birth to a retard only increase by fifty percent."

"I love you," he said, to the shadows of her feet, and he sounded like the new father trying to convince himself that his bloody, gooey baby was lovely by saying, "He's beautiful."

On New Year's Eve, Sam was at Beth Israel thinking about the words used to bestow luck. She and Josef had had a fight the night before and she hadn't seen him since. It was stupid, she knew, to worry about traditions and blessings, but somehow their separation tonight—she at the hospital, he at a party—felt less unsettling than the fact that they hadn't wished each other a happy new year. In the bustling, meticulous hospital, it felt as though every step of any process had to be taken, or the whole thing would be ruined. There was less staff on duty than usual, and frequent phone calls were made to other hospitals checking on the likelihood of a midnight delivery. Mothers showed up throughout the day with phantom contractions and the doctors reluctantly sent them home. It was her last day of filming.

Around dinnertime, a nineteen-year-old gave birth to a beautiful baby girl with a full head of red hair. When the baby was cleaned off and placed at her mother's breast, Sam asked how she felt. The girl never took her eyes off the baby, staring as though she expected it to disappear. For once, Sam thought the camera was getting it all. The girl said, "I feel like I gave birth today." She didn't say it as a complaint. It was just that she knew no other word for the experience she'd just gone through. Sam realized her film would have been far better if she herself had had the experience of birthing a child—that her understanding would have come through in every frame she shot. She told herself she had no business making this film, that it would suck, that she would fail. Then she breathed, and calmed, and told herself it would be okay. She wasn't sure which to believe.

By 11:30, the New Year's tension was palpable. The word was that Mount Sinai had two mothers who were likely to give birth at any time, and even St. Mary's claimed they had one who was ready to pop. Nothing much was happening at Beth Israel. In a few separate rooms, women tried to concentrate on their breathing while doctors came by periodically to measure dilation. "I'd kill for a 12:01 delivery," Sam heard a nurse say. "I hate those pricks down at Mount Sinai."

By 11:50, it was clear that a first-time mother named Lucinda was the only hope they had. She was having cold flashes, almost-continuous contractions, and she'd vomited twice. Her doctor, a bossy, powerful woman, had been rubbing her uterus for thirty minutes, and now, without the slightest bit of empathy, told Lucinda that she'd entered into the transition phase, the hardest part of labor. Soon, the snarling began, and Sam didn't think delivery could be far off. The doctor, however, ordered Lucinda not to push, not even to think about pushing or about things related to pushing. She was clearly trying to delay the birth—whether for medical reasons or to win the contest, it was hard to tell—but when the head appeared, she sighed irritably and told Lucinda to push. The baby, a seven-pound, three-ounce boy, was born at 11:57 PM. Lucinda cradled her new baby, whispered over and over that she loved him, but that birthing room held the air of failure.

Mount Sinai delivered a healthy baby boy at 12:04, extending its streak to four years.

Sam got home at two in the morning. The subway ride had been full of New Year's revelers, some passed out and others singing sad songs on their way to hangovers. In their apartment, the landscapes were back up, as beautiful and mournful as she'd remembered. It felt like the music of her home had changed from circus jingle to funeral dirge. Next week's *Village Voice* was naming Josef a "Voice Choice Hot Emerging Artist," though no one at the paper had ever seen the landscapes.

She poured herself a glass of wine and wondered if her life would change now that there was no animal sex on her walls. During their argument last night, Sam had dragged Josef over to the "Rules for Living." It was a stupid argument, concerning whether avocados contained the good fat or the bad fat, yet it had prompted Josef to say the thing he'd said to her all along: "I'm just not sure." It wasn't a matter of being sure, she had argued. It was making the damn relationship work without any guarantees—just moving forward and building a life. She had written, "Stop resisting and join the human race."

When Josef got home, Sam was on her third glass of wine. He poured himself a glass and sat beside her on the couch. It was his couch, a heavy wooden relic covered in blue and white images of the sea, so they called it "the yacht," and it was on the yacht that they'd made love for the first time—sitting together on that couch, she'd first told him she loved him (ten months before he'd say the same to her).

"How was the party?" she asked.

"Good," he said.

They sat together for some time, drinking in silence. He finished his wine and poured himself another glass. On the way back to the couch, his leg brushed against hers; "Sorry," they both said.

"Are you still mad at me?" she said.

"I'm not mad, Sam. You?"

"I don't know," she answered, and she didn't. She didn't know what she felt. She wanted him to be different, that's all.

He said, "I'm not mad, it's just . . . I don't know . . . I've been thinking about us and . . ."

"Don't," she said.

It wasn't necessary to hear what these words would sound like. The #1 rule on the list said, "Talk about everything. Leave no words unspoken." She'd make an exception here. There were ugly uses of language, imprecise and damaging words. She thought about the corny, joking way doctors held out umbilical cords and scissors to husbands and said things like, "Free this baby," or "Release your child from its bondage." It wasn't the right way to welcome someone into the world. She'd leave their breakup as silent as the meaning of her film.

"Samantha," he said.

"The filming is done," she said.

He nodded.

"It's weird, because I have all this footage now, like eighty hours of it, and I still don't know if I've found anything. I think I have, though."

And she tried to figure it out, aloud to Josef, as she'd always done. He'd been her best friend for so long that she relied on telling him her ideas to understand them herself. She wanted to articulate the secrets she'd uncovered, knowing that soon the breakup speech he had planned would be there in the room with them, drowning everything else out.

She told him all she could find the words to tell, surprised at the rush of discoveries waiting to be uttered. It seemed so clear: her life without Josef, the shape of her film, the miracles surrounding a birth. The discoveries, however, began to fade away as soon as her words died out. Over and over again, she discovered and lost, discovered and lost, and so she spoke more quickly, trying to catch up to them before they disappeared. Josef let her speak her way through it, never interrupting, and it seemed as if he were interested.

She described the moment when that bossy doctor had tried to stave off the delivery of Lucinda's baby. It had been fascinating, the force of her certainty; she'd held her hands over Lucinda's womb in a gesture of absolute defiance: *Not yet!* And the way everyone in the room seemed to hold their breath as though they were all under the doctor's spell. The unblinking eyes, unbreakable silence, the warding off of things to come.

LOOKING AT ANIMALS

RAYMOND KNEW ALL about invisibility. It was what had made him so successful during his thirty years at *National Geographic*; in jungles and deserts, beside rivers, in grasslands—he could get closer to the animals than anybody else. He'd photographed Siberian tigers from just a few feet away, blending into the tundra and chanting to himself, *I am nothing. I am nothing. I am nothing.*

Four months ago, Raymond retired to Morrisville, North Carolina, a stone-still town with one video rental store, a diner, some bars, and a concrete park with a patch of too-green grass. He chose Morrisville because his sense of the place was that people let one another be. It was small enough that everyone knew his name, but at least they didn't feel the need to use it too much.

The business with Greg Phillips started like this: Sitting on his front porch one night, Raymond spotted a big kid of about sixteen crouched under Bob Henderson's bedroom window. Something about the kid—how comfortable he looked, how calm—told him that Greg was neither a burglar nor a pervert. His curiosity was benign; he was, like Raymond, a watcher.

After that first night, it was a simple matter of doing what Raymond had trained himself to do. If he looked thoroughly enough, he was sure to find Greg leaping over one of those idiot wooden fences that didn't keep anything out that wanted to get in, or perched under a window, or listening at a closed door. Greg wasn't particularly careful, didn't slink or crawl, and Raymond could tell he believed himself invisible. Which was funny, because he sure as hell wasn't. The kid made all sorts of mistakes, wouldn't last a minute in the Serengeti without the animals sensing him, but then again he wasn't all that bad either. It wasn't right, probably, to hold Greg to his own standards. After all, there was such an art to imperceptible observation.

Greg smelled more strongly of curiosity than any animal Raymond had ever come across, a scent like fresh mushrooms, spearmint, clean sweat, and so it was easy to plot the course of his wanderings. In doing so, in crouching behind trees across the street from Greg, or even hiding a few feet away beneath the very next window, Raymond has learned more about Morrisville than he ever would have in a lifetime of conventional looking.

For instance, it was common knowledge that kangaroo rats could copulate thirty times a day, but it came as a surprise that Mr. Locke—a stout, quiet man—was a male kangaroo rat in training (his wife, as willing a kangaroo rat as Raymond has ever observed). He's seen Dr. Liebson, a dignified doctor-turned-lawyer, spilling tears onto old photographs and saying, "Mommy," over and over; Mrs. Hartz winking at her reflection and whispering, "You're one hot ticket. I want to fuck you." He has heard their shouts, the inhuman growls, the confessions, has noticed that the more intimate the secret, the louder it was spoken, as though these people wanted to be heard—wanted someone to tell them their desires were normal, their fears justified, that they were A-OK. It wasn't particularly complicated, Raymond thought; all animals have a call for when they're lost or afraid. You couldn't possibly follow a pack of wolves for long without recognizing the connection between howling and loneliness.

If a lightning bolt flashed during one of these expeditions, Raymond knew what people would see: a stocky teenager hunkered down in the boundary between inside and outside. They would see a weather-beaten man watching the boy from behind a car or up a tree, and they might wonder what sort of a game the two were playing.

Raymond wondered this as well. He was fifty-six years old and spent his days watching Greg and his mother, Pearl. The hairs on his body were gray. His skin was gray. His eyes had dulled to gray.

Yet.

Yet, he was surprised that now, in his retirement when all he'd wanted to do was watch the movies he'd always been too isolated to see, and sleep in a warm bed every damn night—it was strange that now, for the first time, he would suddenly acquire an interest in people.

Today, Pearl made oatmeal with chopped almonds and bananas. She sprinkled on cinnamon and sugar, scooped it into large bowls, and stirred in butter and honey. Coffee brewed in a silver pot on the stove. Raymond was right outside their kitchen window, and if he hadn't trained his stomach not to growl, he might have been afraid it would give him away.

As always, their radio was on. It was old and wooden, sat on the nightstand in the bedroom she and Greg shared, and it was never silent: talk shows, Dixieland, baseball games, weather forecasts, local crime reports. Greg and Pearl didn't talk much, so it was the radio more than anything else that provided the sound in their lives. And Raymond's too.

When they did speak, it was inevitably about Cob, Greg's father. It was a familiar story, and Raymond thought Cob was a good example of the inconsistency of human fathers. Some of them spent hours a day with their kids, while others, like Cob, just left one day and never came back. Within all other species, fathers were more consistent: either they all stuck around, or they all left.

Pearl drank her coffee and watched Greg spoon oatmeal into his mouth. She said, "You eat just like he did."

"Jesus, Mom, how many times are you going to tell me that?"

"I know, honey, but it surprises me every time."

"Well, it shouldn't."

Despite the aroma of coffee and the buttery cinnamon of the oatmeal, Raymond noticed Greg's scent; it wasn't just curiosity, there was desperation as well—a biological need to flee. In the photograph he could have taken (had he remembered his camera), it would be obvious that Greg and Pearl were in need of drastic transformation. Both of them scooping the delicious-smelling oatmeal into their mouths without tasting: Taste was often the first thing to go when an animal gave in to a wound or disease, but Pearl and Greg were far too healthy for such surrender.

"Greggie, honey, when he left it was like my soul walked away and wasn't ever coming back."

"Why don't you be a little more dramatic."

"Stop picking on me," she said.

"I'm not."

"You are. You're picking on me because you don't know what it's like to be alone. You don't know the sound of an empty house because I'm always here protecting you from it."

"What are you even talking about?" he said, brushing his curly hair from his eyes. No matter how often Pearl cut it, his hair thrived like a weed.

"You just want to escape from me," she said.

Greg didn't answer, but his face was that of a Florida panther glancing at a young jackrabbit with apparent indifference. To Raymond, the face said, *I'm deceiving you.*

Pearl sipped her coffee. "Greggie, I know everything you think."

"That's not true," he said, standing but then sitting back down.

"You can't ever leave," she said.

There was an empty chair at the table and Raymond imagined himself in it: some coffee, a wife, a kid. He thought about filling in the space left by Cob's departure, but it wasn't a very pleasant thought. Growing up, Raymond and his mom had their own empty chair. She'd gesture to it when speaking of his father, as if he were still sitting there.

He knew enough about love to know he didn't want any. Early in his career, near Iceland, he had photographed a female ceratioid fish about three feet long with a five-inch male fused to her abdomen by his lips and tongue. All the male's organs had degenerated except those needed for reproduction. Her blood flowed through his body. It was ugly as hell, but they'd done it, the goal of all lovers. They'd succeeded in becoming one.

Sometimes Raymond followed Greg to school. Greg picked his nose in class, thinking himself unseen; he ate alone; he muttered to himself. Neither his jeans nor the collared T-shirts he wore were big enough for his large frame, so he'd slump his shoulders and try to diminish his bulk. Once in a while, one of the other kids wanted to fight him after school, and Greg would bare his teeth and pummel the unfortunate kid into the dirt, but for the most part he was ignored. Raymond would think about his own high school—the other kids unsettled by something within him, instinctively keeping their distance—and how absolutely certain he'd been that, if he stood up on his desk and shouted, nobody would have noticed. That he'd have sat back down like nothing had happened.

Today Raymond stayed with Pearl. She walked out to the back porch to smoke the one cigarette she had each day, and he positioned himself just a couple of feet away. The cigarette was probably the only secret she kept from Greg, and she smoked it in deep inhales and exhales, slowly and with great care, as though it were the one thing in her life that was hers alone.

After the cigarette, she went into the living room and made the same phone call she made every day. "Number 3332 back on," she said, and within minutes of her call, the phone started ringing. Raymond had never known that psychic phone lines existed, and certainly wouldn't have guessed that a phone psychic could be as confident and specific as Pearl. "You will quit your job and move to Detroit," she told someone. "You will find love, but the man will have no thumbs." She was honest to a fault. "You are not following your dreams, nor will you ever." "Your husband is cheating on you, and if you confront him he'll leave. He'll be dead within a year, anyway, so I suppose it doesn't really matter."

Lying there, concealed in the kitchen pantry, Raymond could imagine these callers wanting to believe everything she said, even the bad stuff—wanting to discard all responsibility. It was what he envied most about animals, how their lives were ruled by instinct, with no choices to make or regrets to have: the way turtles and salmon just returned to the spot where they were born as though programmed to do so, spiders spinning the webs they must have dreamed before hatching, how honeybees sculpted honeycomb. How comforting it would be, he thought, to see your life as a set of points you were bound to reach, no matter what—to be able to say, for instance, *Yes, lurking in this kitchen pantry is exactly where I'm supposed to be*.

In Alaska, Raymond once lay down in the empty den of a wolf pack he'd been observing. At the time, he wasn't sure why he was doing it, but he'd come to understand that he was hoping to be accepted into the pack—a slower, clumsier member, but still a member. Unfortunately, wolves had no natural predators except humans, and no amount of food or affection, and certainly not the idiot dreams of a photographer, could ever offset that fact. Lying in their den that day, after three months of observation, he'd known he would never get any closer.

Today, while Pearl and Greg were out shopping, Raymond went into the bedroom they shared. There were two single beds separated by a nightstand (the radio on top of the nightstand), two dressers, yellowing walls, and a large mirror facing the beds. Of the higher primate species, only human babies slept alone. Parents were meant to respond quickly to the cries of a baby, which, in earlier times, would have alerted predators. Greg, however, was far too old to sleep with his mother, and his bed, when Raymond lay on it, reeked of all that desire to escape. Raymond watched himself in the mirror, an old, gray man curled up like a little boy. What would it be like, he wondered . . . a room so barren, your mother's sleeping body reflected in front of you, the sound of her breathing?

And the sound of the radio, of course (right now, big-band swing). How tempted he was to turn it off! To hear silence where it had never been. He would have just clipped a wire and been done with it, but he wasn't sure he understood Pearl and Greg intimately enough to predict what sort of effect silence would have on them. Still, he scooted their beds as far apart as they would go.

Looking into all those houses, Greg was bound to have opinions about what he saw, and so he wrote letters telling the people of Morrisville exactly what he thought of them. Even Raymond had received such a letter a few weeks after moving in.

Greg liked houses where the doors and windows were open and the wind blew through them in gusts of cold air. He liked lawns that needed to be mowed, and filthy swimming pools. Dog collars made him angry, as did white walls, eight-foot ceilings, and unused fireplaces. He liked to smell pies and cakes baking, and to hear the people inside talking about how big their slice was going to be. At least, Raymond thought he did.

For the most part, the people who received Greg's letters would shake their heads and try to figure out which of their friends was playing a prank. Raymond would watch them search the letter for clues to the author's identity, ignoring what Greg was trying to say. For some, though, the letters provoked action. They'd paint their walls bright colors, open up the windows and doors. The Augartens placed steaming pies on their windowsill, hoping Greg would help himself. He didn't.

He wrote his letters late at night in the basement, and Raymond had to hide there for five hours, waiting—pure hell on his knees and back, even worse than tracking snow leopards in Tibet. The basement housed a desk, a lamp, boxes of old photographs, and in its seclusion, the radio was no louder than a hibernating bear.

When Greg finally did come down, he got right to work, expelling words onto the page in a way that reminded Raymond of the explosive daily urination of the African tortoise. Then he sighed far too deeply for a kid so young, placed the letter into the desk, and climbed back up the stairs, the opening basement door releasing festive sounds of radio polka.

Raymond allowed his breathing to speed back up. He blinked for the first time in almost two hours. There were so many tricks to invisibility and sometimes he was sure he knew them all, which made him both proud and uneasy.

Greg's letter was addressed *Dear residents of 38 Adrian Street*. It told them that every time their front door opened, the stink of sweaty isolation was unleashed upon the world. He suggested bleaching the floors and even putting a thimbleful of bleach into their bathwater. He complained that their television was far too loud and turned on too often. *Why do the two of you live together when you so clearly hate each other?* he asked. He acknowledged that they were *outstandingly old*, but still suggested divorce, and if that didn't work, suicide.

Raymond didn't believe a word of it. All that misdirected hostility. He could remember his own jumbled anger at Greg's age: not really anger so much as rage cut with woundedness. He could see now that had the opportunity arisen, he too might have suggested suicide to an elderly neighbor.

Cob. It was Cob's fault. And his own father, Dirk. Dirk and Cob: such hard and thoughtless names. He'd once thought it was just males; they were all pricks and nothing could be done about it. But then, how to explain emperor penguins at the South Pole? Fifty degrees below zero, Mount Terror in the distance, the windiest spot on earth: There must have been ten thousand male penguins huddled together, eggs balanced on their feet. They wouldn't eat for four months, losing half their body weight while the female penguins were out feasting in the Ross Sea. If a baby hatched before its mother got back, the emaciated male would regurgitate penguin milk to feed it. He'd seen male wolves regurgitating food for their pups, male ostriches leading lions away from newborns. Hell, male seahorses even got pregnant and gave birth. No, it wasn't just a cursed gender.

Here was a fear of Raymond's: If a young male chaffinch were raised without hearing the song of an adult male chaffinch, he would never develop a full song of his own. The chaffinch needed a male around as a kid or he'd wind up singing a kid's song his whole life. So maybe it didn't matter if Raymond could come to terms with the way he'd spent his fifty-six years, or if he tried to help Greg and Pearl. Maybe there were limitations to what could be worked through.

He tried not to think about chaffinches too much.

Last night, Raymond glimpsed where all of this was going. They were positioned—Greg on a second-floor balcony and Raymond lying flat on the roof of a van—looking in at Mr. Gannon, a nice man who walked his two cats on a leash. He and Raymond often spoke about felines or the weather, and frankly, Raymond wouldn't particularly have cared that Mr. Gannon took such pleasure in films of young men copulating. But seeing it, seeing this middle-aged man lying on his floor, a cat on each side, a bottle of moisturizer, box of tissues—it would be difficult now to speak to him about low-pressure systems or the peculiar grooming habits of Japanese bobtailed cats.

He'd seen it all with animals: male hedgehogs urinating on females in the moments before intercourse, the way monkeys picked their asses, smelled their fingers, peered deeply into warm piles of shit. There was a limit to what witnessing secret lives could teach, and a limit to what Raymond wanted to see. This—this *watching*—was all he had to look forward to: the same secrets, the same ordinary/bizarre acts. In thirty years, he'd be exactly where he was—still climbing trees and crouching under windows, still just watching.

He'd start small. Today, while Pearl and Greg were out shopping, Raymond fixed their refrigerator—a Freon problem, nothing he couldn't handle. He anchored their coatrack to the wall so coats wouldn't droop to the floor anymore. Jimmied the radio (Johnny Cash singing) so it couldn't get so damn loud. He sat on the back porch and thought about how small changes could make their lives better, then ran—or as close to running as he'd done in ten years—to the nursery and bought wildflower seeds. Pearl should have wildflowers. He scattered them in the backyard, slipping out in the moment before they came home.

In his letter to Raymond, Greg complimented his open, screenless windows. He thought the animal photographs covering the walls were Raymond's family photo album, and while Raymond hadn't ever thought about it that way, he now agreed. Greg was disappointed, however, that given those great photos and the fresh air, Raymond seemed like he was probably *a doddering crackpot. Must suck*, he wrote, *to be an old man living alone in a tiny house.* For most of the letter, however, Greg went to great lengths praising Raymond's lawn figures.

Raymond had geese, gnomes, turtles, a dragon, pirates, plastic schoolchildren frozen hand in hand, Oriental small-clawed otters, various apostles whose names he'd forgotten, elves. He often arranged them into elaborate scenes, competitions of gnome versus biblical figure, mammals versus reptiles.

Raymond wasn't sure if it was as Greg had written—were the figures really *a miraculous realm of possibility*? But he did know that in every country in the world there were plastic, wooden, and metal imitations of all things alive. A carved animal was noiseless and scentless and far safer than the real thing. Plastic children couldn't be wounded, and there wasn't the slightest bit of guilt attached to the smile of a ceramic mother. In fact, they all smiled, and it was deeply satisfying, the unwavering smiles—how one figure would never harm another.

Today, Raymond arranged his figures so that each one faced its opposite. He couldn't say why, for instance, a monkey was the opposite of a turtle, or a dolphin the opposite of a wooden businessman, but they just were. He didn't even notice Greg watching him.

"Those supposed to be opposites?" Greg said.

He was leaning over Raymond's picket fence. Behind him was a great oak, and beside that, the neighbor's Dumpster. For all he knew, Greg had been hidden away in different spots, peering at him all morning.

"That's right," Raymond said, feeling, for some reason, as though he'd been caught talking to himself, aware as well, that these were their first words together. "How did you know?"

"It's obvious."

"It wouldn't be to many people," Raymond said.

Greg shrugged. "Yeah, well, it's pretty creepy how many of them you have." In his letter, Greg had said, *I like the dances they do with one another, and the games they play. I like that each of them has so many friends.*

"You don't like them?" Raymond said.

"I don't know—whatever. A few of the opposite sets are wrong, though. Gnomes aren't the opposite of elves, snakes are. There's others too."

"Help me arrange them," Raymond said.

"I don't think so."

Raymond had so much to tell him, mostly warnings so Greg could avoid ending up like him. Words, though—he didn't know the words a person would use to say these things, and wouldn't have understood if someone said them to him. A howl he would understand, a warble—the snarl of a mother bear protecting her young. There was more meaning in that snarl, he thought, than in all of the words he knew.

"Well, see ya," Greg said, turning to leave.

"Wait, Greg . . ."

"How do you know my name?" Greg asked, with a look of confusion but also recollection. Raymond recognized it as the look an animal gave when he'd made a mistake and let himself be seen. The look said, *So you're the one.* Animals sensed when they were being followed. Prey had evolved to trust this sense, but for humans these types of intuitions weren't vital, and so weren't honed. So while Greg most likely suspected something, Raymond was almost positive he couldn't name what it was. He bolted without waiting for an explanation.

Saying Greg's name was just stupid, so stupid in fact that Raymond wondered if it really was a mistake. He understood that people often acted unconsciously, and maybe this error was actually an attempt to get caught. He couldn't be sure—it was just one unbidden word after all. He knew, however, that saying Greg's name out loud had felt good, had been like saying, *I know you, Greg Phillips. You and I aren't strangers.*

Late that night, while the rest of Morrisville slept, Raymond watched Greg rearrange his lawn figures, from opposite sets to sets closest to one another. The figure of Judas paired with a hyena. The businessman and the squirrel. Lion and the otter. A plastic brown puppy set beside the old iron wolf. Did Greg know that dogs were just domesticated wolves? Or that the Homo sapiens of today were domesticated Cro-Magnons—smaller, weaker, gentler? Humans were evolving away from savagery, toward empathy. We have real fear now, he thought, not just an instinct for survival. He imagined this fear as something useful, helping to give meaning to things, to name the stakes.

Here was a fear: forget about success, or finding true love, or leading "the good life." What scared Raymond was the thought that he'd failed to lead a life at all, any kind of life—that in his invisibility he wasn't even a part of the world.

It took a lot of attempts before Raymond was forwarded to Pearl's psychic line. He must have talked to fifty "psychics." Strange, so many people out there just waiting to tell him about himself, as though his secrets were floating on the air for anyone to snatch up.

"What would you like to know?" Pearl asked.

Raymond sat with his cell phone in the hollowed-out middle of a hydrangea bush in Pearl and Greg's backyard. In the spaces between the flowers, he could see Pearl speaking into a phone of her own.

"Tell me everything you know," he said.

"You watch people because you have nothing of your own. In your dreams you're still a child. You're afraid you've never made a decision that wasn't based primarily on fear. You think you're not equipped to live in this world."

"I sound like a real pussy," he said. "It's true about the dreams, I suppose, but I think you're off on the rest."

"People don't often like the things I tell them."

"No, it's not that. I just think you got me wrong."

"It's not easy to hear the truth."

"Pearl," he said, "I'm not sure if you're one to be preaching about fear."

"Who is this?"

Raymond watched the confusion come across her face, and then the fear, and then the anger. He was glad there was anger because it showed that she hadn't given up completely. She looked out her window, but he knew she wouldn't see anything. The shelter he'd carved in the hydrangea didn't provide a hundred-percent coverage, but hell, even at his clumsiest he was still a professional.

"Tell me why you're still alone, Pearl?"

"Enough about me. I know more about you than you've ever known about another person."

He said, "Just because someone left you once, they won't all leave."

"Who is this?"

He settled back comfortably into the bush. "A mother's function is to prepare her child to leave. Greg leaving you is the surest sign of your success. If you let him go, he'll come back, but if you force him to stay, you'll lose him."

"Who is this!"

"It's Cob," Raymond said. "I'm never coming back. Find someone else to love."

He hung up, propped his feet onto a thick branch, and

watched what he'd done. She screamed, and cried out, threw the phone against the wall. *Today*, he thought, *Raymond Adams helped Pearl Phillips.* She needed to know this stuff—it wasn't any good sparing her.

It was past midnight, and Raymond had been staring at the small blinking light for almost an hour. He wouldn't even have had an answering machine, but it came with the phone. He thought, *Who in the world would want to talk to me so badly that they'd leave a message?*

He pressed the blinking light and listened to a man advertising a dating service. The voice, though, wasn't of a man, but of a disguised boy who said that living alone was no way to live—that lawn animals and photographs could only get a person so far. He listed a phone number for the dating service and a Web address where animal lovers chatted with each other.

My God, Raymond thought. *The little bastard is trying to help me.* He found himself thinking about the wolf pack in Alaska, the one whose den he'd entered—how the day he boarded his small plane, ten miles from where they usually roamed, he saw them, the whole family, hidden behind a snowbank. He had observed them for so long, he'd lain down where they lay, and now they'd come to say goodbye. He felt that same kind of acceptance now.

He didn't write down the dating service number, though, or the animal chat room address. These things didn't inter-

est him in the slightest, and he hoped he'd been more accu-
rate in guessing what Greg needed.

Raymond changed the washer on Greg and Pearl's leaky
bathroom faucet. He tightened the screws and balanced the
blades of their wobbly, unstable ceiling fan. Then he got
hungry—it was midafternoon and Greg and Pearl were at
the laundromat—so he took a few bites of leftover meatloaf
out of a Tupperware in the refrigerator, had a swallow of
milk from the carton. On the radio (quieter since his repair,
but still audible) there was a talk show people called for
advice. *You're on the right path*, the radio woman said. *Keep
doing what you're doing.*

It wasn't a sign, Raymond told himself. Though he wanted to believe it, how could this . . . this handyman routine
be the right path? How could it lead somewhere good, or
normal?

Still, in the night he scattered firefly eggs in their backyard and weather-sealed the back porch, so that when the
rains came, Pearl could smoke her one cigarette without the
threat of rotting wood. Airborne, blinking lights would tell
her she wasn't alone.

Tonight, Raymond felt Greg watching him in all the rooms
of his house: under the living room window, at the front
door, in the shrubs out back. He could have sworn he'd
heard Greg hidden behind his couch last night, and two

nights ago, Raymond had even walked toward the window to invite him in. He was too late, though (probably wasn't a good idea anyway): he had seen Greg's too-large shadow bounding away like an overgrown baby gazelle.

Raymond sat on his couch reading a pamphlet for a "lively retirement community," which Greg must have slipped into the pocket of his pants. The community had bridge leagues, tango and flamenco nights, something they called "mixers." Raymond laughed at the photographs of those gray-haired men and women sitting around bingo tables wearing absurd grins. He certainly didn't want to move into some lively old folks' community, but he did want to read the pamphlet, and let Greg see him reading it.

Yet how strange it was to know you were being watched. Raymond was aware of every gesture he made, his nose itched constantly, and he couldn't stop thinking about what his life must look like. Good or bad, he didn't know, and it probably didn't matter, anyway. He himself had never watched an animal in order to judge the quality of its life. It was just important to see the shape of it, the layers and borders—to understand what the thing was made of. The shape of his life must be an awkward, disconnected form outlined in pale, tentative lines, but it was no worse than anyone else's. It was a wonderful gift to be watched.

Earlier today, before finding the pamphlet, and before eating homemade chili out of a Crock-Pot in Pearl's kitchen while she and Greg watched television in the living room (was she making extra food these days or did he just imagine it?), Raymond had run into Pearl and Greg in the supermarket. He'd been reading the ingredients on a box of cereal, and when he looked up, there they were, Greg pushing the cart and Pearl leading.

"What's up, Raymond?" Greg had said.

"Oh. Hello."

"He lives on our street," Greg had explained. "The house with all the animals on the lawn."

Pearl knew the place. It was a happy-looking house, she said. She asked him about the cereal box he'd been reading. Full of all kinds of crap, he explained. They laughed when Greg said the crap was the best-tasting part.

"So," Pearl said, "what is it that you do?"

It wasn't an easy question and he hadn't known where to begin. He started to speak, then stopped. How to go about explaining all the things he'd seen—how to put his life into words? A certain delicacy of phrasing was necessary, an eloquence he knew he didn't have. This incapacity for expression: He imagined it as the fibrous plug that grew in the rectum of hibernating bears to keep them from defecating in their lairs. Like the bears, he knew he'd have to summon enough force to shoot out the plug.

He thought about wooden radios and phone calls predicting the future, lawn figures and letters written to strangers. How to explain the difference between a voyeur and an observer? He considered isolation and all the ways he'd climbed deeper into it. What he'd done, he'd done out of kindness; if nothing else, they should know that.

He understood, however, that it wasn't necessary for him to explain. Pearl already knew why her bed had suddenly stopped squeaking and why flowers were sprouting throughout her yard, and Greg was no idiot. And even if they couldn't put into words what they knew, they sensed plenty and didn't need any of his half-cocked definitions to fuck it all up. And what was amazing—what was the kindest thing he'd ever seen—was that their faces held the glint of smiles, utterly without disgust, like the reflection of curious eyes in the dark.

He picked up the box of cereal (he wasn't afraid of food additives!), and headed toward the milk aisle. He was careful not to glance back at them, knowing that in looking at animals, the most important thing for both the watcher and the watched was to play stupid, to act as though there was nothing connecting you—to never give up the secret that you weren't strangers.

DISORDER
DESTROYERS

APE FORAGED A corn niblet from his wooly moustache and was eagerly considering it. I shook my head at him. Meanwhile, the Cains, perched around their coin-filled Jacuzzi, pretended not to spy on us. After a summer of working for Disorder Destroyers, I was used to clients watching us work, but the Cains' constant lurking was as extreme as their mansion's clutter problem. In the three days we'd been there, the Cains had watched everything—the emptying of the kitty litter room, the shoe room, the shoe box room; removal of their corkscrew collection, handsaw set, their many caviar spoons, tapas pans, and fish poachers. Mr. Cain was the CEO of a corporation in which our boss, Dr. Tony, suggested we invest heavily. Other than the lurking, they looked like a family you might see on a television show about country clubs: all of them— mother, father, and eight-year-old daughter—tall, blond, and perpetually dressed in white.

Dr. Tony called what we did Litter Management. It was his business and he had lingo to describe it all. Our clients weren't Westchester County psychotics who collected trash; they merely exhibited one or more symptoms of Object Obsession Disorder (OOD). Ape and I weren't meatheads who tossed boxes into Dumpsters, we were Litter Specialists. It said so right on our shirts, alongside the company logo, which also appeared on our pants, Dumpsters, the truck, and was even embroidered on the baby-blue handkerchiefs Dr. Tony carried. The logo showed a giant with Ape's bone structure shaking his fist at a cowering sack of trash. Disorder Destroyers was called in when a litter problem—be it magazine collections or rotting mountains of food—became a genuine safety hazard.

For the record, however, our clients *were* psychotic, albeit interestingly so, and Ape was, unquestionably, a meathead.

We were in the grand foyer, a dozen chandeliers raining down thousands of watts, litter everywhere.

"We could do the attic," I suggested.

"You seen the attic?" Ape said.

"Backyard?"

"They got a pot-bellied pig out there. And a peacock. And a billy-goat-looking thing."

"It's an alpaca," I said.

"Never heard of it."

Normally, we couldn't get to the back of a client's house before first clearing away the front, so there were no decisions

to make. The Cains, however, had fifty rooms to distribute
their mess, plus a three-acre backyard, its massive pond
filled with rowboats, inner tubes, and Canadian geese.

"Kitchen?" I said.

Ape nodded. It was a good idea to clear out kitchens,
since grateful customers would frequently offer us cold
drinks or bake lemon bars in their newly liberated ovens. Dr.
Tony had tagged almost everything with red "Annihilate"
stickers—it was mostly stacks of take-out menus, phone
books, and rusty cooking gadgets—so we just tossed it all
into the Dumpster. As a general rule, the stuff people
couldn't bear to part with had no actual value. A few of the
Cain things, however, had the yellow "Eradicate" stickers,
which meant we loaded those items into the truck for Dr.
Tony to sell on consignment. Occasionally, Dr. Tony had us
bring the clients' favorite piece of litter—a prize marlin, or
a mysteriously cuddly teddy bear—into the backyard so they
could kick the shit out of it, his theory being that sometimes
the only way to let go of the objects in our lives was through
cathartic acts of brute violence. There was a special sticker
for this, a black one that said "Genocide."

As we worked—me stacking mail, Ape hauling portable
meat smokers and Snack Masters to the Dumpster—Ape
started in on his favorite subject, his wife: in this case, how
she had a cyst she was thinking of removing but that he was
all for keeping. ". . . and just because it's called a 'cyst,'" he
was saying, "doesn't mean it's any less a part of her, or that

I shouldn't love it. Would I take a surgical laser to her plump, delicious thighs? Or her doughy belly? I don't think so, buddy."

"This is a cyst we're talking about?" I said, but he wasn't listening.

I'd met Ape's wife once: fuzzy, dumpy, toothy; "How you doin', guy?" she'd said to me. For Ape, however, she was the only important thing in the world. He'd tell me I was wasting my time studying our object-obsessed clients. But he was wrong. Sure, these people were pathetic—too much money and too little faith in the power of a good spring-cleaning— but they were also the most openly wounded and intriguing people I'd ever seen.

There was less than three weeks until my junior year started, and I felt much more like an actual historian here, digging through strangers' kitchens, than I ever did reading textbooks at Hampshire College. In my ancient history classes, all we had to go on were the artifacts cultures left behind—their goblets and primitive weapons, figurines of gods—so studying the objects of the present didn't feel so far off.

While Ape listed every possible procedure for removing the cyst, and the Cains positioned themselves behind an outdoor pizza oven, I gave in to curiosity and delved into the kitchen litter. When I first started at Disorder Destroyers, I looked through every box and bag before throwing them away. Dr. Tony had encouraged this curiosity, but warned that my need to spy on people's stuff was a distant cousin of their need to collect it in the first place. He'd initiated a policy called One for Ten, in which I was allowed to open up one box for every ten I threw out. He assured me that if everyone with a psychosis could successfully quell their desires nine-tenths of the time, they'd make the important transition from full-fledged aberrant to harmless kook with a fetish.

It was really difficult, however, to look through the Cain trash with the Cains behind their oven pretending not to watch me. I feigned an untied shoe and got a look at the largest collection of restaurant and bar matches ever, so I feigned another untied shoe and, shockingly, the next box was box two of the same collection. Then I had to take off my hat and feign wiping off sweat, so I could feign dropping the hat to see if there was a third box of matches, which there wasn't. (This one was filled with Chinese take-out packets: soy sauce, chopsticks, napkin, fortune cookie.) I hauled the matches to the Dumpster, erasing all those years of traveling, eating, and drinking, hoping the Cains had taken photographs as well as matches. Then I took the chopsticks, and then two armloads of oven mitts tied with twine, and by then I was due for a reward, so I feigned a leg cramp, sat down, and sifted through a carton of books, one of which was *100 Gifts for the Man Who Has Everything.*

A picture was beginning to form of the Cains. With their exotic animals and functionless rooms, their depressed maid and sixteen-mattressed bed (the bedsprings held together with

bungee cords), their chiseled good looks. They were people
who came from money but were still compelled to make more.
They believed that by surrounding themselves with objects,
they'd be safe from the loneliness that plagued others.

Or maybe not—it was just a theory, after all, but then, I
was the one sent in to rescue them, so even my most untest-
ed theories held the weight of authority. I picked up my box
cutter and considered the pile.

"Looking for something?" Dr. Tony said.

Open boxes lay scattered around me; nobody could sneak
up like him. It may have had something to do with his size,
an inch under five feet tall, and that was with the booster
shoes he wore. Also, he was such a chameleon—dressed to
blend in to the particular color scheme of the house in
which we worked. In the case of the Cains, he wore a series
of tan suits, brown shirts, gold fedoras. I swear, he disappeared into the crown molding.

"No, I was just . . ."

"Larry, please don't further your disgrace by telling me
some sort of horse-cock tall tale." He was doing that thing
where his face was happy, but his whisper sounded homicidal.

I opened my mouth but nothing came out.

"Oh, Larry, my young protégé, what are we to do with
you . . ." and he described how vulnerable the Cains were
during this process, how the slightest thing—for example,
seeing me rummaging through their stuff—could set them
off. He chronicled the many diagnoses he'd made in the

weeks before Ape and I were called in: alcoholism, lachana-phobia, obsessive-compulsive disorder, a whole bunch of abandonment issues; he'd even diagnosed the daughter as dyslexic, and simply wasn't convinced they were stable enough for the long-term demands of living litter free.

I didn't like letting Dr. Tony down. Unlike most of my so-called "professors," Dr. Tony was the sort of guy you could actually learn from. I would have apologized, but he'd just have lectured me about the colossal pleasure I'd feel were I to murder the sorts of behaviors that compelled me to apologize. He often used words like *murder* or *massacre* to describe the actions necessary for proper psychological health.

I got back to work, annoyed that the Cains had seen my chastisement, but also thinking it was only fair. Fine, they knew I got scolded, but I knew that Mrs. Cain's gym bag contained a five-pound bar of chocolate and a case of butter cookies, that Mr. Cain's medical records included the term "chronic bleeding hemorrhoids," and that little Tanya Cain took pills (placebos, but they seemed to be working) for her bed-wetting. Still, they were camped out behind their oven gasping in a throaty way each time I threw a batch in the Dumpster, so I took to chucking things extra hard, delighting in the sounds of breakage. I dumped the books, and then load after load of stuffed Glad bags, one of which, when smashed into the sharp Dumpster corner, crunched as if it housed bones. When I shot-putted a box filled with Gandhi photographs, one of the Cains shouted,

"Oh, that's just *enough!*" and Mrs. Cain came out from behind the oven, flashed me a look of contempt, and dove headfirst into the Dumpster. She emerged gracefully, the box of photographs tucked beneath her arm. "You won't say anything," she said to me, walking toward the front door.

"You're wasting your time!" I called out. "Dr. Tony will find it." I turned back to the other two Cains, but all I saw were four hands clutching the brick edges of the pizza oven as though it were a lifeboat.

Living at home was strange. My parents couldn't seem to keep track of my life anymore, questioning me about people I hadn't seen in years or tests I'd passed two semesters ago. "You've become too private," they'd tell me, but really they'd just stopped paying attention. I'd tried to fill them in on my summer job, explaining Dr. Tony's theories about objects, but their eyes glazed over and they asked what was on TV later. There was a time when we'd eat dinner together every night, but since they didn't seem to care, I installed a lock on my bedroom door, and didn't come out.

After all that snooping through other people's objects all day, I couldn't help but study the things I still had lying around. Boxes of GI Joe figures, photographs of me towering over kids at my Poughkeepsie Middle School graduation, the coins I'd once decided were lucky and, though they looked normal enough, still couldn't bring myself to spend, butterflies I'd captured, suffocated, and then pinned to cardboard frames.

Mostly, however, I looked through the "vital objects" I'd taken from clients' homes all summer. A vital object was the single item that heralded a person's transition from "messy" to "afflicted." A worthless plastic fork placed into an empty box because another box of worthless plastic forks was already full was likely to be a vital object. I suppose there was no way to confirm that, say, the second copy of *Moby Dick* was what did it, or the busted spatula someone refused to throw away, but Dr. Tony thought my instincts felt right, said I had a sixth sense for sniffing out the beginning of downfall.

His faith in me meant a lot; this was a guy who could read people at a glance. We would go into the houses of people who had been dangerously OOD for twenty years, in therapy for ten, and after a week with Dr. Tony they'd be filing police reports for the childhood assault they'd blocked out and throwing away immense collections of cleavers and hand-spun nooses. He was the best because he could single-handedly diagnose and then solve the problems that would otherwise have wrecked lives.

And speaking of power: vital objects strewn about my bed; how amazing did it feel to surround myself with the very things that had sent other people over the edge!

There was one benefit to living at home. Lying on my bed, I had a perfect view into our neighbor's window. Growing up, however, the only thing to watch was Mr.

Stevenson working at his desk. Occasionally, I'd turn off my lights and hunker down, hoping to get a glimpse of him fishing for boogers, but mostly I'd just shut the blinds and hope he couldn't see in. The Stevensons must have moved out while I was away at college, and Mr. Stevenson's old office was now the bedroom of a girl about my age who seemed to do nothing but undress and dress. And undress.

I never said anything about the box Mrs. Cain rescued, but by the fifth day, I was beginning to think other dumped items had disappeared as well. Also, some of the stickered objects had had their stickers taken off. I described my suspicions to Dr. Tony, who grabbed me by the shoulders and herded me into the board-game room, where he shut the door and began stacking boxes of Monopoly and Chutes and Ladders up against it. "Extra insulation against would-be spies," he whispered. When the games were sufficiently stacked, he repeated what he'd said when we started at the Cains'—that in all his years of giving the three Fs (fisting, fucking, and foul play) to Litter Accumulation, he'd never seen a case as downright virulent as theirs.

"Anyway," he continued, "you're spot on about the reclaimed and de-tagged litter. Someone in this house is engaged in a quiet but ultimately malignant mutiny, and, mark me, Larry, mark me!" He pulled me close, his breath cold and piney. "I'll excise the heart out of the tumor that is Dumpster raiding."

One time, Dr. Tony drew me pictures of the sixty-four different emotions human faces were able to show, an astoundingly specific collection of subtle differences. For instance, one face was identified as "Liar who doesn't know he's lying," while another said, "Liar who acknowledges the possibility he might be lying." Put those two next to someone who was "telling the truth, but fears he may be lying" or one who was "telling the truth, but wishes he could think of a lie," and I, for one, had a hell of a time telling them apart. What I'm saying is, the guy could read volumes into the tiniest of gestures. Nobody was equipped to conceal things from him, not even things they themselves couldn't name.

Read me, I wanted to ask, but knew I never would. *Show me what I'm concealing.*

"Who do you think it is?" I whispered.

But he wasn't listening. He was already on the case.

The next few days were something of a blur, from the house to the Dumpster, house to Dumpster. In the midst of all the dumping, however, I overheard Mr. Cain ordering carrier pigeons over the phone and saw little Tanya Cain rushing through the back door, shopping bags swirling around her. Ape debated nonstop with a nonexistent doctor about the foolishness of cutting away a benign hunk of his wife, eventually concluding that the cyst was a physical representation of the love they shared. We finished the kitchen (no lemon bars, no offer of delivery pizza, not an ice-cold Coca-Cola or even a glass of seltzer water), the master bedroom, the daughter's room, and a bunch of the full-of-trash rooms (some of which ended up completely empty). The Cains' eyes followed us wherever we went, and I gave them looks of my own, scornful glares like fishhooks. Dr. Tony brought in a van full of inner-city kids to clear the Jacuzzi of coins, and every time I looked out there, Ape, his head under the water, was grabbing handfuls of coins and throwing them onto the lawn where the kids were killing each other in an effort to collect the most. Animal welfare workers came in and took the wildlife away, and then a professional cleaning crew disinfected the animals' turd field (soon to be a rock garden per Dr. Tony's recommendation). The peacock stayed, since the Cains swore from the beginning that if Mr. Feathers went, Dr. Tony would go as well. Dr. Tony, by the way, despised peacocks as "the worst sort of concession to mainstream standards of beauty," and whispered to me that if he had his way all the Mr. Featherses of the world would be too-bright dog food.

"I actually sort of like them," I said.

"You don't like them!" he insisted. "Repeat it with me, please." And so I repeated it. I still liked them, though.

I also liked the maid, a skittish, defeated-looking woman in a black-and-white costume who confined her cleaning efforts to one bedroom in the easternmost corner of the second floor. Whenever one of the Cains would put something there, she'd immediately whisk it away into one of the already-ruined sections of the house. I set an over-flowing box of half-burned candles into her safe haven, and when she cleared it out, I put it back. Again and again. She never said a thing—simply removed it. I speculated that perhaps years of living with the Cains' OOD had whittled away her capacity for anger. But without anger, what sort of life could a person lead? Pushed around, accepting whatever scrap of attention someone offered: if this wasn't the beginning of downfall, I didn't know what was, so I returned the candles to the same room, determined to bring anger back into her life.

I sifted through the Cain litter, searching for the origin of their immense disaster. There were mustard collections, Austrian shaving kits, boxes of pomade, of rubber cement, of colored ice-cream sprinkles, but none of it held the stench of downfall. I was beginning to think I'd lost my gift, or that maybe I'd never had it to begin with. Which was scary, because it seemed like such a valuable gift.

This job had taught me that there were a million ways a life could go wrong: jugs of alcohol ruined people, but so did subscriptions to newspapers, large-screen televisions, and old couches kept around after a new one was bought. The list was probably endless, each person on the planet burdened with one or two things that could ruin them. I wanted the ability to identify everyone's potential downfall, to walk through department stores making diagnoses of those who passed by, occasionally singling someone out for rescue:

If you buy that giant television, you'll sit in front of it all night, every night, and you'll never do any of the things you dream of doing, you pathetic fuck.

A hero.

Here was what I began doing:

I'd hide Mom's keys. She'd search like hell, pissed at her declining memory. Then I'd search along with her—the only thing the two of us did together. Eventually, of course, I'd find the keys, and each time she gawked as though seeing me for the first time. She'd hug me, and we both agreed that getting old sucked.

I'd surreptitiously turn down the volume when Dad was watching television. He was sensitive about his hearing and I'd watch him lean toward the television, squinting his eyes as though seeing were the key to hearing. Finally, after what must have felt like forever, I'd say, "Hey, Dad, do you mind if I turn up the TV? I can barely hear it." "Do whatever you want," he'd say, trying to hide how appreciative he was—how relieved that I'd saved him from having to admit his weakness.

Her fading memory, his loss of hearing: These were the first outward signs of the downfall of their bodies. Someday, she'd blankly repeat her stories over and over and he'd scream, "What?" every time, but for now, I was the only one who understood what was happening. They could only see what I allowed them to see. This was the control Dr.

Tony had, walking into a ruined house and seeing everything our clients couldn't.

Each night I locked my bedroom door and laid out the
objects I knew I'd never throw away: the letters from sev-
enth-grade girlfriends, my lucky coins, the butterflies I'd
killed. I'd also lay out the vital objects of our clients. It was
like exposing myself to deadly diseases; I was impervious to
the things that harmed other people.

I'd watch the girl in the next window—the clumsiest person in the world. Everything she picked up, she dropped and
had to bend over to retrieve. She spent half her life in panties
bent over her desk and bed, picking up and then dropping.
Late one night, she read a magazine on her hands and knees. It
was pitch black in my room and I'd stuck a book between the
blinds so I could see everything. I liked being alone with the
objects and with the girl next door. She was tiny, almost delicate: short blond hair, snail-shell ears, pale snowball boobs.

She must have been open to the possibility that there
was someone in the dark window across from her, and I
imagined that this exhibitionism was a call for attention.
She probably thought her parents didn't love her enough, or
that she was all alone in the world. Sometimes, watching
her, I had the feeling we were connected in some way, as
though, without speaking, we understood each other.

On the morning of the ninth day, Dr. Tony found a hidden
stash. He rushed over to recount the steps leading to his

discovery. ". . . and once I smelt the deceit drifting from her toes, it was a simple matter of reading the text of her face, a clear, eloquent combination of two looks: *I'm hiding something important*, and, *Please don't go into my walk-in closet and find the secret door.* So I went and I found. Incidentally, it's always the feet where deceit is most easily detected, because, of course, deceit actually weighs more than other emotions, so once gravity has his way with it, blammo!"

I waited for him to say more, something more plausible perhaps, but, plausible or not, he had found the room based on the smell of the woman's feet, and in doing so, had once again confirmed that all the secrets of the world were open to him alone. It almost didn't seem fair to pit him against normal people who couldn't find meaning in a twitching eye, a flaring nose, or a sock full of deceit.

The "she" in question here was Mrs. Cain, and the room was big, about twenty by twenty. Except for a narrow clearing, it was entirely filled with all manner of political paraphernalia: books, videos, stickers, figurines. The walls were covered in posters of political activists, mostly Gandhi, striking dramatic rock-star poses as though fasting and passive resistance were sensational and sexy. There was a pewter, a plastic, and a ceramic Martin Luther King, Jr., some wooden Che Guevaras, a Leonard Peltier, and a whole team of Gandhis. In the corner sat an enormous bust of Marx. Dr. Tony said her obsession with political resisters came from her father, a dedicated Trotskyite who'd never forgiven her for dropping out of Bard to marry a businessman. I noticed, however, that none of this stuff was boxed or tagged, so if they were raiding the Dumpster, this wasn't the cache. I was also fairly certain that these weren't vital objects—that the Cains' problems didn't stem from this collection.

I was reminded of that poor maid and her one immaculate room. The thought of emptying Mrs. Cain's secret room felt as cruel as filling the maid's oasis with clutter, yet without any of the fun. With the maid, all that was being destroyed was the room's emptiness (and it really was for her own good), yet here was this enormous, seemingly complete collection. I don't know, I guess the stuff was worthless, but there was no way I'd be able to throw any of it away.

Dr. Tony wanted Ape and me to be there when he confronted Mrs. Cain, so that his insistence that we empty the room seem less like his personal distaste for Gandhi, of which he had plenty, and more the collaborative guidance of the entire Disorder Destroyers team. When she entered the walk-in closet, Dr. Tony took Mrs. Cain by the hand and led her into the secret room. "Oh, dear," she muttered, her face in her hands.

"This can't stay, you know that," Dr. Tony said.

She peeked through her fingers: "How much will we have to get rid of?"

Dr. Tony looked around, seeming to take in every object in the room. "The Rosa Parks bobble-head," he proclaimed, "can stay."

She started weeping—Dr. Tony unfurling one of his often-cried-upon handkerchiefs—and Ape picked up a British convoy truck and made a defeated-sounding engine sputter; I aimed for the toes and inhaled deeply, trying my best to identify the scent of foiled deceit.

That night, I made a discovery of my own. I found that if I got down on my knees near the opening in the blinds, face pressed against the window, I could rub against the wall, and it was as if the neighbor girl was right there with me. I'd changed my mind somewhat regarding her exhibitionism. It wasn't that she was clamoring for attention; she was actually punishing her parents, who had forced her to come home from college for the summer. I'd arrived at this conclusion based on the "Go Wake Forest Deacons" sticker she'd put up on her window, the double lock she'd bolt each time she entered her room, and the tense, vengeful grin that crossed her face at especially erotic moments. Watching her was the best, most tranquil part of the day, and I could understand what the Cains' maid felt in her immaculate room, or what Mrs. Cain had lost when Ape dismantled her secret collection.

She'd sprawl across her bed in underwear and a half shirt, tickling her thighs and outlining her nipple with an index finger. The wall felt better than it should have, and I knew that both of us were feeling what it was to be together.

By day twelve, I'd begun thinking in similes, deciding finally that emptying the Cain house was like emptying the ocean in the rain with a plastic soupspoon. We'd lift and unload, lift and unload, emptying the Dumpster every three hours to keep them from reclaiming their stuff. Dr. Tony held daily Object Obliteration meetings with the Cains where they meditated on all the ways they hated their objects. Judging from the screaming, there must have been quite a few. Some boxes were reclaimed—at least I was pretty sure we sometimes threw the same thing away twice—and it seemed that every day Dr. Tony found another hidden room crammed with litter. Still, the Cain house was growing more full rather than less; their accumulation was moving faster than we were.

Strangely, this defeat was somewhat pleasurable. Despite knowing how devastating Object Accumulation could be, it was still getting difficult to simply shit-can the Cain hoard. Even if all they had in their lives was this crap, maybe it wasn't insignificant; I mean, the terrible gloom on those chiseled faces—like it was bodies we were dumping.

What I began doing was taking a box of, say, bike helmets from one room, and, on my way to the Dumpster, I'd veer off, take a series of stealthy turns, and stash them away in a chest of drawers I'd previously scouted out. It wasn't right that everything be eliminated.

Ape, Dr. Tony, and I were puttering around the Cain attic, Ape lounging victoriously on top of a mountain of baby clothes, me looking through a box of hats, and Dr. Tony muttering to himself in the far corner, working on a new strategy. Earlier, Ape had high-fived us, punched us in the arms, and announced that the cyst had been officially saved. Dr. Tony had asked my opinion about tagging all the remaining Cain items with a "Genocide" tag, so the Cains would be preoccupied with killing their old objects, rather than accumulating new ones. "I don't know," I'd said. "I guess it could work."

It was day fifteen, my last day of work. Ape had lessened his work pace, since it seemed the Cains accumulated objects at approximately the same rate he dumped them. He wasn't making any progress, so figured he might as well take it easy. As for me, I just couldn't bring myself to throw away any more of their stuff.

The attic must have been a hundred by a hundred, the entire space filled with overflowing boxes. It was the ground zero of Object Accumulation. I stood, frowning at my reflection in the freestanding wooden mirror, a gray fur shapka perched atop my head. "What are you doing?" I asked the reflection.

Ape looked up at the sound of words: "I know," he said, "this is the best job ever." I took off the shapka and dropped it to the floor. "Yesterday," he continued, "I spent three hours watching *Gandhi* with Mrs. Cain. She was like, 'Abraham, stay, relax.' There was this huge bowl of salted peanuts in the shell. She kept repeating that Ben Kingsley was put on earth to play Gandhi."

"It's pointless," I said. "We're wasting our time."

"Wow, Larry, you're looking at this all wrong. For the past two hours I was napping in that room with all those beds bungeed together. I was like rolling over and rolling over for miles but I never hit the wall, and here's you standing around dressed like a fur trapper. Last night, I got home and felt like I'd spent the day at a ballgame or something. I wasn't tired at all and my fingers tasted like peanuts."

I could hear Mr. Cain calling out to Dr. Tony. Before long, he entered the attic and the two of them sat down on boxes of *TV Guides*, Dr. Tony explaining his new plan for the Genocide tags. Mr. Cain nodded eagerly, his checkbook seeming to appear in his hand as though conjured. And as he wrote out the check, I tracked the changing map of his face, an almost audible expression of ecstasy. There was nothing he'd rather be doing than handing money over to Disorder Destroyers. "Ape," I whispered, "you see that?"

"See what?" he said.

But the look was gone just as quickly as it had appeared. I suspected, however, that I'd just glimpsed the beginning of the downfall of this project. Though I wouldn't be around to see it, Dr. Tony would someday admit defeat at the Cain house. We hadn't healed them of anything; on the contrary, we'd become their newest collection.

That night, in my bedroom, I lined up my collection of vital objects: the cracked ashtray I'd found in one client's home;

the bent fork stored in a jewelry box; a tattered pair of boxers squirreled away in a paper sack. Talk about inviting disaster: When you decided that your faded, torn underwear was worth saving, how could you possibly throw away anything ever again? Tomorrow, I'd make it back to Hampshire in time for Tuesday drink night at the Alibi. But before the Alibi, my roommates and I—a bunch of guys I hadn't talked to since school let out—would sit around discussing our summers. I didn't know what I'd tell them.

How, for instance, would I describe our defeat at the Cains'? I myself wasn't sure what I felt. Passionately ambivalent, I suppose, as though it were simultaneously a victory and a defeat. A victory and defeat of what, however, I didn't know. Earlier in the night, my parents had taken me to dinner, had one too many Bud Lites, and told me that they wished we were closer.

"I've been home all summer," I'd said. "Why are you just saying this now?" They'd shrugged, grinned, and then turned their attention to the cleanliness of their silverware. I might as well have been alone.

I ran my hands over my pillow, my coin collection, over the stolen pair of ripped boxers. And for a second I could see these things as an alien might—as the mysterious talismans they were. It was so easy to accumulate objects because each of them was a small miracle. Were I left on a deserted island for a thousand years, I still couldn't have made a simple piece of paper or a pair of jeans, let alone an ultrathin plasma television or a breathable microfiber. For some reason, it was objects that solidified the most meaningful events in our lives: the birth certificates and photo albums, wedding rings, the urn full of ashes.

In the midst of these reflections, the light across the way turned on and the girl next door came into her room wearing a blue summer dress and flip-flops. In the corner of her bedroom were two suitcases just like the ones I had out. She put her head in her hands and it seemed she was crying. When she looked up, red-eyed but without tears, I smiled, pointing first to my suitcases, then to hers. She watched me blankly.

I tried returning to the objects but she continued to stare. When I turned to her, she pointed to her feet and took off the flip-flops, then pointed to me. I could feel my heartbeat increase. I was wearing the brown Timberland boots I'd worn every day this summer. It had gotten so that my feet were more comfortable with the boots on than off. She was watching and waiting, so I took off my shoes, my socks. She no longer looked sad, or maybe she'd never been sad. I guess I had no idea how she'd felt or was feeling. She took off the dress, and her black panties and bra were so skimpy that they seemed chosen more to contrast with her pale skin than to actually cover anything.

She pointed to me, but I wasn't sure I was capable of moving. My mouth was dry and I may have been shaking—could hardly get my shirt off, fumbled for what seemed like hours with my belt and zipper. Her bra went next, and then her panties. It was the first time I'd seen her completely naked. She lay back on her bed, watching me and waiting, and I didn't know what to do . . . felt forced into it, as though she were physically there removing my boxers.

She was rubbing herself, so I did the same, but I couldn't feel anything. It was like I wasn't even a part of my body. I pulled and pulled, but nothing. Her stare was completely unnerving, so I looked away, focusing on my collection of school yearbooks. From the corner of my eye though . . . this beautiful woman, mouth opened, teeth gritted, rubbing and staring.

I pulled, I stroked, but there was no way I'd get off with her watching. I'd have killed for a pair of sunglasses, or a mask, or a blindfold, yet she was bouncing around like an epileptic. I could see how ridiculous it was to have thought there was some sort of connection between us. I knew nothing about her except for the color of her discarded clothes, the color of her blanket, her watchband, her suitcases. I thought about Ape's intimate knowledge of his wife's cyst, and it didn't seem so stupid anymore.

I tried to focus on the foot of her bed, but in shifting my gaze, I suddenly caught a glimpse of my own reflection in the window. And what I saw was a twenty-year-old with the beginnings of a belly furiously whacking off to a neighbor he'd been spying on all summer, the expression on his face like a rapist in a movie. It didn't look anything like me, or at least anything like I thought I looked. Yet there it was: me.

I focused on her glistening knee, far away from both her gaze and the reflection of my own. There was no way out now, no way to stop her staring except through orgasm. I pulled as though my life depended on it. It occurred to me that the lonely, pathetic face I'd glimpsed in the window might be the shape of my potential downfall, and that from then on *it* would be the face I'd see in the mirror, maybe hovering behind all the faces I tried to plaster over it. I pulled. I wiped away a tear. There was nobody in my life I felt close to. It hurt, but I was getting there. I focused on her thighs, on her quivering breasts, her painted toenails.

Then there was a knocking, which I quickly realized was coming from my bedroom door. "Larry, can we come in?"

It felt like plunging. I didn't know if the door was locked. They fumbled with it. I must have appeared petrified, inanimate, like a sculpture depicting masturbation. The girl next door took it all in, or maybe took none of it in, massaging and gyrating, her eyes locked onto mine, the door slowly opening, and I clutched my blanket and the edge of my bed as though, behind them, I could disappear.

KING OF
THE FERNS

THE WORST THING I ever did was the worst thing any fern can do. I broke the Rule: I reached out and caressed Peter as he crawled by. I knew it was wrong, but he is such a good and stunning child, and I needed to feel the warmth of his soft skin against my flourishing leaves. Peter screamed and cried—it was a glorious song!—and I was elated. But the Rule is the Rule and really shouldn't be broken.

I believe in logic and in rules, but without passion what are we? And on that day I asked myself, am I a fern or just some unfeeling ficus? And I knew. I am a beautiful and powerful fern. I am a vital part of a family on the verge of collapse, but I have hope. I am not without resources.

I suspect that I'm the King of the Ferns, but then, who can really tell?

My wife's name is Kimberly, our son is Peter, our dog's Don Carlos. I am Jonathan.

The third worst thing I've ever done was to kill my dog. I'd just torn open the last of twelve rejection letters for the novel I'd sent to twelve publishers. This was eight years ago. I was twenty-six and too stupid to realize that no matter how many publishers I sent it to, it wouldn't get published. At the time though—clutching that last rejection—all I knew was that I'd wasted three years writing a masterpiece nobody would ever read. Enraged by the world's inability to recognize genius, I walked into my apartment and Hazelnut started right in, jumping and barking. "Fuck off, Hazelnut," I muttered, pushing her away.

I take full responsibility for what happened, but I think Hazelnut should have recognized that the tone in my voice meant I was losing control—I had lost it before. I walked into the bedroom with her nipping at my calves, and sitting on my bed were the chewed-up corpses of my brand-new hiking boots.

I just reacted, anger and frustration channeled into violence. I reared my foot back as hard as I could and the sound of my heel on her snout was sickening. She yelped and went down and never came back up. Imagine lifting your collie into a trash bag.

The second worst thing I've ever done was marrying Kimberly, a woman I didn't love. We met in grad school shortly after I killed Hazelnut. She was twenty-seven, the most beautiful woman ever made, and staring at her naked body, making love to her: these were the most amazing moments I'd ever experienced. It was just too good for my cruddy life, felt like something one man steals from another, so I instinctually protected it.

Look, I don't know about any excuses; she's a gorgeous, intelligent woman and she loved me. I was an ex–fat kid accustomed to masturbating into cantaloupes; I thought, hell, what do I know about love? I know that undressing her fulfilled every perversity that had ever flashed through my head while fucking overripe melons, and I reasoned that this, perhaps, was love.

My husband's name is Jonathan, our son's Peter, our golden retriever is Don Carlos. I'm Kimberly.

The worst thing I've ever done was taking pride in my beauty and using it to destroy men. The fact is, many men fall in love with me just by looking. When I smile, men don't even see a human being: They see a tan, tall body, which for some reason stays toned, and big boobs, which for some reason don't droop; they see green eyes, straight blond hair, and a small, pointy nose. They're certain that this face would never hurt them. In my teens and early twenties, I broke as many hearts as I could—flirted with everybody, led on anyone who would follow. I'd burn their absurd notes that threatened suicide.

Jonathan is easy to be around. He has a great body and the most amazing, beautiful penis I've ever seen. It's big enough that I can really wrap my hands around it, and it's flawless—smooth skinned, none of those weird bulging veins, perfectly straight and utterly dependable. Also, his balls are as big and round as golf balls (I don't like those puny, mismatched balls). He cooks for me, listens to me talk about my students, and when I read his books, I know that he's a genius. I need him and he needs me.

Yet Jonathan stares out of our living room window for hours on end. In town, he imagines that every couple is more in love than we are, and every man more attractive to me than he is. Movies and love songs have ruined him for the real world.

He always wants more: more love, more intensity, more me.

~

The worst thing I've ever done, I haven't done yet, but I decided this morning I will.

I was at my desk writing, and Kimberly rushed by as she does every morning, her breath thick with coffee. She kissed me on the ear and told me she loved me. Then she bent over and kissed Don Carlos on his floppy ear, and in the same rushed tone, told him that she loved him.

She was dressed in a tight skirt-suit, and her legs were like bronze. Kimberly teaches high school art—has her students look at the same paintings year after year. When we see these students in town, they watch her with equal parts awe and hunger. I'm certain that a large number of them remain in our town after graduating simply for the pleasure of catching an occasional glimpse of her. Sometimes, they'll say to me, "How's your, uh, 'book' coming?" and then they'll smirk because certainly they've never heard of me, and neither have their parents.

I stay home with Peter each day, take care of him, and write my books. I guess you'd call them literary fiction, which means that every three years, I publish another book that no one, other than a small community of readers, will ever read. Unless I'm out with Kimberly, I go completely unnoticed.

But I just can't do it any longer: can't watch people watch her, can't wonder what she's doing all day, wonder if she's talking to other men. I can't raise Peter in a home like ours. For him, I'll give her up.

The worst thing I will ever do is to take Peter and run somewhere so far away that I won't even be able to recall how it felt to know she was mine.

You see? You see how close we are to withering away?

For more than a year, Peter has held us together. Were we a body, Peter would be our heart. I don't have a heart, by the way, because I'm a fern, which is funny if you think about it, and I'd laugh if I could laugh, which I can't—still a fern—but then there's Peter. Even Don Carlos loves him—so much that his wish is to devour him. Don Carlos would never kill Peter, though, because somewhere between hunting squirrels and licking his balls, he knows that to kill Peter would be to kill the entire family and he needs us just as we need him. A family must be unrelentingly protected—UNRELENTINGLY—because . . . because what? Because anything could destroy it. Because we are fragile. Because cutting the wrong vine would kill us. Consider this:

For a short while, there was another fern directly across the room from me. I sang all day and night to this fern, a song for Power—imagine the merciless pounding of a hurricane. Now personally, I'm not a fan of direct rainfall, but I'll bet my terracotta pot that I could take on anything some hurricane threw my way! However, this new fern was neither strong enough nor beautiful enough to survive my song. It weakened and begged me to stop (wretched pleas that continue to torture me, if you must know), but what choice did I have? This fern was incompatible with our family. Its presence was something foreign, like a transplanted organ, something we as a family had no choice but to reject. Its death was distressing but necessary, and I believe the sacrifice I made was worthy of the King of the Ferns, who, maybe, I am—me!—but maybe not.

～

I look out our living room window and watch the trees—so much uninhabited, wild space. We are surrounded by ten acres of forest and Don Carlos is free to roam as far and for as long as he wishes. Occasionally, he'll come home bearing a squirrel or a rabbit, which he presents at my feet, but usually he stays close to the house. Once, Don Carlos chewed up a pair of my leather dress shoes. I did not hit him. I do not hit anybody. I do not lose my temper anymore.

Sometimes, at night, I, too, roam this forest while Kimberly sleeps. I can only say it's a compulsion, like picking a scab. Something about the disorder, the dirt, something about the darkness. Now and then, I'll scream into the night, expelling everything within me. Who knows what I'm becoming? I like the feel of forest mud between my toes. I enjoy the smell of deer shit, a scent like the essence of earth, only earthier and rotten.

I like to perch outside our bedroom window and watch Kimberly sleep. Asleep, her face takes on the same slight smile as when she stares at herself in the mirror. I imagine that, like me, she dreams of her image. I know it's pathetic, but the fact that I'll never have anything as beautiful as Kimberly makes it feel impossible to leave her.

I am the first son in the third litter of Bootsy, implanted within her by Bert. My owners are the Franklins: Jonathan, Kimberly, and Peter. I am Don Carlos.

The second worst thing I ever did was the chewing of Jonathan's black leather shoes. I knew it was of all importance to him that I not chew his shoes, yet the scent of them—

the warming sweetness, the salt—was maddening. I was unable to resist. Jonathan almost never leaves his shoes where I can get to them, and when he catches me sniffing an unguarded pair of shoes, the putrid scent of shame drifts up from his body. It is the fear that if I succumb to my desire for his shoes, he will lose control of himself and cease being a man. He fears the animal within him and for this I have no respect. When he mounts and breeds with Kimberly, he is more man than animal and it should not be thus.

I see him late at night, running barefoot through the forest. I trail him as he screams and claws his way up steep inclines into spaces without paths, sometimes pausing to inhale from a fresh pile of dung. His tracks frequently indicate that he's running on all fours. Yet, when he returns home, when he has placed his muddy clothing in the wash and bathed his pale body, the pathetic scent of shame drifts from him and I am repulsed.

Occasionally, I bring Jonathan a dead squirrel or a rabbit to remind him that he is an animal as we are all animals and that cowardliness and inaction can only lead to death. He sits most of the day with a computer and his words. He is all thoughts and words. Despicable. Sometimes he stares out of that godforsaken window, his face turning red, and he removes the charcoal portrait of Kimberly from the wall. Then he strikes the wall with his fist. There are many holes in the wall, many exposed wires. Yet does he show Kimberly what he's done? No. He puts her portrait back, pretending that he hasn't done what he's done. He is nothing but a bitch.

Yet he is known as a killer (he once killed one of the collies) and there is respect in that. Also, he is my owner, and I should be loyal to him above all else. Do you know what, though? I would like to kill him. I believe he could be provoked into a death fight. His teeth are very sharp and it would be a magnificent battle. The warmth of his blood on my snout, weariness of well-fought combat, Kimberly understanding once and for all just who is the dominant male in our clan: the glory!

⌐

I don't believe I'm capable of looking her in the eye and telling her that Peter and I are leaving. So while she's been off at work, fueling the masturbation of her students, I've begun writing a history of our relationship together. I'm hoping that if she reads about us through my eyes, she'll understand the inevitability of this escape.

Peter is my boy—has spent every day of his childhood with me, comes to me when he wakes from a nightmare, holds my hand crossing the street. He's mine.

⌐

The worst thing I ever did was biting little, tasty Peter. He was crawling along the floor and Kimberly was in her bathroom spraying herself with a certain perfume that makes me want to mount and breed with her. I suddenly caught the scent from him—the freshest, cleanest meat—so I bit him on his ankle until he cried, then bit his little arm and he screamed and continued screaming. He bellowed like a wild animal and it brought me inexpressible pleasure to bring sorrow to such a pretty creature. Also, I liked that, though he was a Franklin, he had no mastery over me. We were equals and strength was all that separated us. Until he could walk, I would bite him, never hard enough to draw lifeblood, but enough to cause his delicious animal screams. I was never caught.

I fear him now. He grows larger each day. I detect that the infuriating scent of fear drifting from his scrotum will someday be replaced by vengeance, the most bitter, acrid scent. I fear most that, were I discovered, the Franklins would cast me out of this family and I would be alone. That I fear this small and helpless child sickens me. It forces me to consider what I have become in my many years of comfort. There is a growing desire within me for the fluffiness of carpet and the warmth of our home. My teeth are dull, my rump often aches. That I should hunt and roam far and with much savagery! That I should once and for all find the courage to battle with Jonathan! It is a battle he, too, desires—I can smell it—but there would be much blood, and even if I tore him apart, I might yet have to leave this home. Though I desire it with much intensity, I am not certain Kimberly would accept me into her bed.

Within Kimberly there is no fear. She lives as she wants, confident that all is hers for the taking. Kimberly breeds with other men. I smell the sour scent of their mating drifting from her clothes and skin. There are many men and the smell makes me want to mount and breed with her.

—

I don't consider it a sin. What I do with other men has nothing to do with Jonathan. They are an amusement, while he is half my life. To put it simply: Yes, I'm attracted to Jonathan. However, occasionally I need a truly beautiful man. I need, for instance, the symmetry and magnificence of two perfect bodies wrapped around one another. And I need the look on a stranger's face when I disrobe and he recognizes I'm every fantasy he's ever had. It's not simple vanity. It's a need.

I often stand in our living room and watch my reflection in the mirror. I know how this will sound, but I'm just stating a fact: I should be out of Jonathan's league. Everywhere we go, people stare at us and wonder what I'm doing with him. It wouldn't bother me, except that he stares at me and wonders the same thing.

Look, I love Jonathan. I love the heck out of him, but it's like he wants to possess every last bit of me. He wishes for a love he would die for, where instinctually he'd throw his body in front of a bullet headed for her heart. He would never die for me, but is that really a problem?

⁓

I'm writing chronologically. Our story began in a graduate literature class. Every man in the room was watching someone, so I turned and saw a woman without any imperfections. If I could somehow arrange to have sex with this woman, I thought, to see her face every morning and to walk around the world with her beside me, I'd never be lonely again.

For some reason, she was smiling at me.

⁓

I sing my songs for everyone. Peter has nightmares of plants leaping upon him and dogs chewing his limbs, and so I sing him Comfort. I sing for Kimberly, standing in front of the mirror. When she and I are alone and she watches herself, I sing with everything I have—the song for Desire—and during these times I'm convinced that she can hear the strong, high pitch of my chant, the steady, rising tempo, and as she watches her reflection and hears my song, she runs her fingers along her body and I sing. These are erotic moments in this fern's life, but because I believe the King of the Ferns should be a decent fellow, I'll omit the details. (Think hot, though. Hot, hot, hot!)

Like Kimberly, Jonathan stares—not at himself, but out the window onto a world he's struggling to shed. He secretly fancies himself a lion, which would be a reason to guffaw if I could actually guffaw. He believes the mistakes he's made are the result of a wildness within him, so he writes, considering writing an exercise of the mind. Yet his inability to accept his compulsions—to honestly record his desires—clouds his writing, and this is the reason for his limited success.

I'll tell you what he desires: Kimberly, stuck in a pot beside yours truly, where he could water her and admire her, and know that she would never, ever leave her pot. I would welcome the company.

When he and I are alone, I sing the same song for Desire but also the song for Escape—an inferior song in both its absurd quietude and the jarring dissonance of its rhythms—and I believe he hears me and is unable to leave, his eyes alternating from the window to the charcoal portrait of Kimberly, back and forth, his hand furiously stroking his stamen.

They don't even realize the influence my songs have over their lives—probably imagine that their fears and compulsions come from within and their swings of mood are brought in with the wind. I probably am the King of the Ferns.

⁓

I've been working on our story for a week and am almost finished. I've put in every conversation I can remember, every argument, every agonizing day spent wondering where she was and who she was with. I've even included the secrets—

how she picks her toes, wipes up the sauce on her plate with
fingers, the way she incessantly scratches her crotch.
Without her nearby, nobody will ever notice me again, but
still, she's human and I'm not stupid for leaving her.

⁓

"What are you thinking, Jonathan?"

We're in bed, and I'm lying on top of the covers in a new
aqua bra and matching panties. The color makes my skin
look even tanner, but Jonathan's pretending to read.

When we first met, he couldn't keep his eyes off me. In
fact, the first time I saw him, he was staring. We were in a
graduate literature class and I was smiling at this guy behind
him, Tony or Timmy or something, who I'd just begun sleeping with. And there he was, in the corner of my eye: this
artsy-looking boy—John Lennon glasses, scraggly brown
hair, intense blue eyes—staring with his mouth open as
though he'd never seen a woman before. To be honest, I was
totally into Timmy or Tony because we'd done some things
the night before I'd never done with anyone, and I wouldn't
even have remembered Jonathan had he not approached me
after class and nervously asked to carry my books.

"You want to carry my books?" I asked.

"I want to carry your books," he said.

"Go ahead." I began stacking stuff into his arms—the collected Shakespeare, the huge art books, my sweater, and for the
first time ever I walked through campus totally unencumbered.

"I'm thinking about Peter," he finally says. "Does he really love us or is it just that he needs us, or is there even a difference?"

"Of course there's a difference," I say, and I'd show him if he'd look over and touch me. I'd show him love and need, and all the places they overlap. I'm not sure where his head is, but it's nowhere in this room, certainly not on me or my silk underwear or even on the cheap cologne Theodore wears and I was afraid Jonathan would smell.

He says, "There's no difference."

⸺

Jonathan is a fool and a coward. There she is, splayed out half naked, the scent of desire—musk, cinnamon, albacore, fresh moss—drifting from her open legs, the scent of another man's desire coating her body, and he speaks to her of love and does nothing to overpower and reclaim her. If only I could walk on two legs and talk, I'd jump onto that bed, tear out his throat and then I would chew her salty, moist undergarments and mount and breed with her. Then I would lie upon that great bed and she would scratch my itchy belly and I would be content. However, the instant the scent of her desire reached me, I would once again mount and breed with her, for it is in this way one holds on to a female.

Jonathan should die. He is neither a worthy man nor an acceptable master. He's no better than the spot of deer shit on the tip of his nose or the hardened crust of another man's semen coating Kimberly's appetizing buttock.

~

"What are you thinking, Jonathan?" she asks me. What do you say to that? I'm thinking about whether it was worth it. During our time together, did I ever meet a woman I could have fallen in love with? Could she tell how enslaved I was to the idea of Kimberly? Did she sense that, after Kimberly, I would have been embarrassed about the way she looked? Did I miss my chance? Stupid questions.

Still, there is Peter, so it wasn't a total waste. Peter took the best of our features and will end up smarter, happier, and more beautiful than either of us. He has Kimberly's too-bright eyes, her milky skin. Like her, he realizes he's beautiful and understands that people will go to great lengths to see a smile spread across his face.

So I tell her I'm thinking about Peter, though really she couldn't care less. She just wants me to look at her. But I can't look without touching. For seven years, I knew it would end, but still I fucked her and told her I loved her. I can't fuck her now and leave her tomorrow. I am not an animal. I am not a slave to my desires. An animal is incapable of anything as complicated as falling in love, so I don't look. But even if I am an animal, if all I can do is eat and fuck and kick dogs, then fine. I can still care for Peter; even animals care for their offspring.

I lie with my back to her, and in the reflection on the closet mirror I see Don Carlos watching us with a pink boner. I'll tell you something: I'd like to bite Don Carlos on the face. He's certainly asking for it. He doesn't stare at me with that dopey look other golden retrievers give you, but with this tight-lipped taunt, and I want to show him that I'm more than he could handle. I'd get down on all fours and bite and claw that fucker to the ground. She can have that fucker, and the house, but Peter is mine.

⌇

Do I regret the killing of the other fern? I do not. Of course I'm aware that this other fern could have served as something of a companion to me. Certainly I experience loneliness. In fact, right now, as I'm singing my songs and watching Jonathan type words into his computer—words whose purpose is our family's destruction—and watching him pick up his son and dance him around on his lap, my singing feels incomplete. I am lonely. Yet how would it have looked to others if I'd settled for the first fern I saw? The King of the Ferns would wait, would be confident, would never settle, and would never, therefore, be forced to break up a family.

Jonathan has crafted the words that will sever everything, but the King of the Ferns would not sit back and idly watch his world unravel. The King of the Ferns would save his family. The question is, with everything on the line, what can I do, whom will I save, what am I?

⌒

I write about the morning I decided to divorce her, write about taking Peter far away, and I write a page about our future. She's not in it.

I print out the story, all seventy-five pages—our whole life together, past, present, and future—and as they come out of the printer, I spread them on the carpet, tiling the floor in sheets of white. I want to try to see the thing in its entirety, everything we've been through surrounded by everything else, like a giant snapshot. I take off my shoes and crawl across our arguments and moments of happiness. I stand up and feel like God or a dead man, finally able to see what my life looks like from above. I pick up Peter and let him crawl across the tale of his birth.

Kimberly comes home from work, takes off her shoes and walks across our story. She sits down in the middle of the pages, saying, "What is this, performance art?" She figures it out soon enough. She reads and reads. I begin to sweat. This is the worst thing I've ever done. I've destroyed something I never had the right to build in the first place.

She looks up at me, disgusted: "What's wrong with you?" she says.

⌒

I say, "What is this, performance art?" The whole floor is covered in paper and he and Peter are crawling on top. Peter's copying Jonathan, so it looks like both of them are reading whatever's written on the pages. So what the hell, I take off my heels and crawl beside Peter. He's pretending to read a page describing a mother giving birth. The mother had planned on natural birth, but because of the awful pain had requested morphine, epidurals, whatever they had. Jonathan often uses bits of my life in his books, so this is nothing new. The drugs made it so I don't even remember giving birth. Just the pain preceding it.

Don Carlos comes over and lies down beside me. I scratch his belly, but he tries to paw my hands down to, I think, his balls. I read a different page describing a man's dissatisfaction. What is it with men and their dissatisfaction? Never famous enough, never enough attention, never loved with enough intensity. This man—in the story—this man is clearly Jonathan. The room seems hot, and I keep reading, moving from page to page, sweat appearing on my body, trying to find something which shows that I haven't spent my life trying to make a stranger love me, instead of just covet me.

"What's wrong with you?"

Let the coward leave! Kimberly and I will inhabit this home without him. Perhaps *this* is my chance to convince her that I am a worthy mate. All I need is the slightest sign from her and I'll tear open his cowardly body and present her with one of his warm organs. His liver. Yes, the beautiful

Kimberly deserves his liver! I lie beside her. The room grows humid, so I bring out my tongue. Perhaps Kimberly and I will breed our own family. I feast upon the floral musk drifting from her succulent body. I wait for the sign.

⌒

Jonathan is typing and then Jonathan is finished and I sing for him the song for Death. He lays his words onto the ground and places the child onto the words and, with me singing—Such beauty in my voice! Such range!—he recognizes the death his words will bring.

Kimberly comes home and sits upon these words of death. Don Carlos walks into the room trailing the scent of Kimberly and lies beside her.

I must stop it. My goodness, am I needed!

Kimberly wants to hear the song for Love because she does not wish to believe the words she reads. Don Carlos wishes to hear a song for Battle because he believes the time of his attack is near. Peter, the adorable child, is afraid of Don Carlos, and wishes to hear the song for Security. But I sing a new song, one I've never sung and one I'm not sure has ever existed. If I can master it, I believe it will keep us together. I am being pulled in so many directions, and how to even describe this song?

The sound is like the Sun itself singing its heat upon us.

If I can understand this song and keep our family in this room together as we should be, I *must* be the King of the

Ferns. And if my song fails and I am not the King of the Ferns and if the Franklins separate, then whom will I sing for? I'll be alone. But for now, the beauty and power of my song overtakes me and I am filled with it. The room grows brighter, hotter, humid even, and moisture collects on my perfect leaves and helps to fuel the singing. And through the force and beauty of my singing, nobody moves! They cannot separate with the magic of this new song upon them. Hear my song now, see how the Franklins are unable to act according to their will! Yet, I'm weakening. The strain of the song may be too much even for the King of the Ferns. Weakening, weakening, weakening—but still impossibly strong! And look at them, motionless, powerless, helpless! I am King of the Ferns! I am King of the Ferns! I am King of the Ferns!

TOP OF THE LIST

WHEN THE MANAGER on duty, Tom Bogan—that prick, that village idiot—tells me that Bruce Springsteen will be seated in my section, I'm not at all surprised. I knew we'd meet someday.

"I'll take good care of him," I tell Bogan.

"I know you will, Mary," he says and gives me a thumbs-up with his cutoff stump of a thumb, which, no matter how many times I see it, strikes me as a less than good omen.

It's five o'clock. My first reservation (a ten-top) is coming in at six thirty, and Bruce Springsteen (and one guest) is coming at eight.

Among the ten servers working tonight at Boston's chicest, sexiest restaurant, John Paul's Bistro, there are nine bachelor's degrees, three from Ivy League schools, and three MFAs, an MA, and two PhDs. You hear sentences here like, "Yale's such a chump institution—my boarding school was far more rigorous." Yet everyone seems content refilling water glasses and dispensing ramekins of ketchup.

I myself have one of the MFAs (in acting) from Boston University. I go to auditions whenever I can, which, lately, is never.

Despite being ex-academics, we cringe when students get seated in our section. We also cringe when black people are in our section, or brown people, or groups of women, or guests with accents of any kind. We like white businessmen and white gay men because these are the only two groups of people who can be counted on to always tip at least twenty percent.

My ten-top, unfortunately, turns out to be sorority girls celebrating a birthday. They're all made-up and high-heeled, and even though I'm only a few years older, they call me *Miss* and *Waitress*. A couple drink amaretto sours, but mostly it's Diet Cokes and extra lemon for the water. It's shared salads (dressing on the side), no truffle oil on the wood ear mushroom risotto, no coconut beurre blanc on the Chilean sea bass, and one passion-fruit tartlet with ten forks—*And could you put like a ton of candles in it and sing happy birthday and everything!*

"You bet!" I say brightly.

I bring all their food at once, and the dessert before everyone's finished. I want them the hell out of my section.

I add gratuity to their pathetic check—$140 for a ten-top!—and place it in the middle of the table. The birthday girl shoves Daddy's credit card in without looking at the total, which means I can run the gratuity scam Will taught me. Basically, you can hide the gratuity you've already added and get tipped twice.

There are more scams in the restaurant business than I would have thought possible, and even more excuses to justify them: *The customers deserve it; the chef's an asshole; the restaurant makes plenty of money; new shoes would be nice.* I used to try out the excuses like fad diets, but I don't really give a fuck anymore. This job takes up a huge part of my life and I'm simply a lot happier making more money.

While my sorority girls are crunching ice cubes and hopefully thinking about leaving, I set Bruce Springsteen's table with reserve wineglasses, a fresh rose, and a crystal snifter with lemon and lime segments surrounding the lip.

I share not only my birthday (September 23) with Bruce Springsteen but also my hometown (Freehold, New Jersey). I dated an Evan for over a year before Bruce and Patti Scialfa chose the name for their first child. Like Bruce, I attended Ocean County Community. My parents, obsessive fans, named me after Mary from his song "Thunder Road," the same Mary of whom Bruce says, *You ain't a beauty, but hey, you're alright.* That part's not very empowering.

I wipe down the L-shaped corner booth with a clean white cloth and, with another cloth, polish the silverware. I want the crystal and the silver to shine beneath the flickering candlelight. I want to hear him say, "Wow, this looks really great," in that gritty worker-man voice of his.

Shannon, a lipstick lesbian who broke the hearts of half the men at John Paul's when she came out, sits down and says, "Mary—oh my God!—what comes with the lamb shank? I told table fifty-five macaroni salad, but now I don't know."

"Gnocchi," I say. "Sweet potato gnocchi with a drizzle of nutmeg cream and caramelized pears."

"Gnocchi are those big macaronis, right?"

"Sort of," I say.

"Thanks," she says. "Love your sorority girls." She runs off.

Will sits down, wearing that tired, angry expression he gets when he drinks. Sometimes I like the look, but tonight it's just sloppy. The bartenders are happy to slip us free drinks, since drunk servers tip out more. I'm one of the few who doesn't drink during shifts. I tried it a few times, thinking it would make me feel like I was drinking *with* the customers, but crouching down in tuxedo pants to drink scotch out of a paper cup felt like something a counselor might refer to as rock bottom.

"Double tip?" Will asks, nodding toward the sorority girls. Shannon is bent over one of them, wiping crumbs from her lap. Will and I have sex now and then.

"I think so."

"Good. Fuck them." He looks over Bruce's table: "New candle." he says. "Crisp linen . . . reserve glasses?"

"Yeah."

"Lemon and lime wedges, Mary? Who sets a table with lemon and lime wedges?"

It's probably Will's chin that makes him attractive. It's the manliest, sexiest chin I've ever seen. Other than that, he's your basic good-looking, though unremarkable, guy. Six feet tall, brown hair, brown eyes. He does, however, shave his balls, something I find surprisingly appealing.

"I want him to like it here," I say.

"Get a grip."

"I know, but I grew up in his city. My parents would sing me to sleep with his songs. Besides, there's more to it."

He waits.

"My first boyfriend was named Evan and he has a kid called Evan and . . . I don't know, other things too."

He coughs and then sneezes.

"Your breath reeks of alcohol," I say, and hand him an Altoid.

"Thanks, Mom," he says, and this seems about right.

An older Euro waves an empty water glass in the air. There's a bottle of San Pellegrino sitting right in front of his underage, blank-eyed girlfriend, but, like Will, our customers are often helpless.

"Table seventy-three needs you," I say.

"I swear to God," he says, "I'm gonna hack them to bits," and he takes out his wine key, unfolds its knife, and goes over.

I get a nine-top of suits, so I smile, showing all my teeth, and tell them in my best Italian accent that I'm Gabriella. Gabriella's a role I played in a community theater production a few years back. It's much easier to respond to flirting old men when they're calling out for Gabriella or Gabbi. And besides, Gabbi likes the attention.

The men buy everything Gabbi's selling: two bottles of the wine she suggested ($90 a bottle), steak au poivre for everyone ($36 apiece), and they all agree to start with the appetizer special, which, Gabbi insisted, "You owe to your tongues to taste" ($16 each).

I punch in their order at the server station. People like to be told what to do—will happily turn over responsibility to anyone who'll take it. That appetizer I just sold them: shad roe with horseradish aioli. Shad roe is the sack—the sack!—that holds the developing fish eggs. It's fish womb. Even people who like liver and sweetbreads and caviar do not like shad roe. But tonight the server who sells the most shad roe wins a bottle of Rioja.

Certain magic words and smiles can not only persuade people to order something disgusting but also convince them they are enjoying it. Bruce Springsteen understands this: in his tight jeans, guitar slung over his shoulder, he's convinced the world that in New Jersey, factory workers drive off in powerful American cars and fulfill all of their fantasies. It's probably the secret of his appeal: Desire + Escape = Success, and for a moment I can believe it myself.

Then I think about the people I know in New Jersey.

At eight fifteen, Bruce walks in. He's in gray slacks and a yellow button-down shirt. Yellow! He's even clean shaven, his hair neatly slicked and combed. It's like Bruce Springsteen dressed up as Bruce Springsteen if Bruce Springsteen had been born in New England and studied mathematics. He's with a small boy who has his strong chin and big nose. Bogan ushers them into their booth with theatrical flourish, offering them his disturbing thumbs-up once they're seated. Evan gives the thumb an appropriate look of horror, but Bruce is a rock.

From the table, Bogan comes directly to me. "I just sat the Boss at table thirty-one."

"Okay."

"I wasn't sure whether I could call him Bruce, so I just said, 'Welcome to John Paul's, Boss.' And then, 'Here's your table, Boss.' I told him I have all his albums, which I don't 'cause his music is ridiculous. I don't think he knew, though. Let's go ahead and send him calamari, mussels, and vegetable spring rolls. I told him you are our most senior server, so don't make me look like I have, I don't know, shit in my brains or something."

Even for Bogan this is a little crazed. I punch in the appetizers with him watching.

He says, "Do you think you could at least pretend you're a waitress and fill up his water glass and take a drink order?"

Up close, Bruce is familiar but unreal, like an invented face from a sex dream. "Hi, I'm Mary."

"Hello, Mary," and it's like hearing my name the way it was meant to be said.

It's you, I think, wanting to bust out laughing and slug him in the shoulder, but also wanting to curl up in a Dumpster and die. I've gotten pretty good at veiling my nervousness onstage—at severing it from the character I'm playing, yet if Bruce looks closely, he'll see that my ears are beet red. "Can I start you gentlemen off with a drink?"

"Can I have a Coke, please?" the kid asks. He really is a little Bruce Springsteen. Give him a guitar, a tight T-shirt, and some booster shoes, and chicks would line up for autographs.

"And a Bud Light, please," Bruce says.

"Coke and a Bud Light."

At the service bar, I watch Marco, the bartender, bent over eating a lamb shank he's scammed and stashed, and not getting my Bud Light. A few paper cups are partially hidden behind the Rose's Lime and grenadine bottles: vodka drinks Marco hooked up for Will, Kelvin, Shannon, and a couple of others. Usually, the paper cups don't come out till much later in the night. Marco is really going at that lamb shank.

"Today, Marco," I call out, pointing at the beer order. "Today!"

I set the Bud Light and Coke down, prepare to launch into the specials, but I can't. Normally, I'm proud of my ability to recite specials—how quickly I memorize them, and the way I can make whatever it is sound as though it's the goddamn tastiest thing I've ever eaten. It's a performance, and I'm good at it. However, while most performances celebrate a person's particular talent, reciting dinner specials to Bruce Springsteen seems to celebrate some fundamental failure. It's how I imagine the performance of stripping would feel.

Growing up, whenever I felt discouraged, my parents would point to one of the many framed posters of Bruce Springsteen hanging throughout our house. They wouldn't say anything, would just point, as though his example said it all—as though, because I was from his town, I could achieve the same success. This was meant to be encouraging, yet from an early age I understood that their faith in me had nothing to do with me. *He* was our source of power, and it was against him that our own lives would be measured.

I walk back to my nine-top of businessmen, take away bread plates to make room for appetizers, fill water glasses, put down steak knives, and pour out the rest of the wine. The man in charge—a man somehow more bald than anyone I've ever seen—nods his naked and shining head toward the empty bottle, signaling he'd like another. Their bill is at $650. I'll make at least a hundred and eighty off this table.

As I'm punching in the wine, Mother and Will come up behind me. Mother is an enormous and beautiful Southern gay man.

Mother says, "So, is he as sweet and nasty as he looks?"

"Did he notice the lemons and limes?" Will asks.

"It's really Bruce Springsteen," I say.

"Is that adorable child his son or his boy toy?"

"Did he notice the lemons and limes?" Will says, more loudly.

I say, "Will, it's like eight thirty and you're slurring."

I turn to Mother. "His son, Evan. He turned twelve last May."

I go down into the kitchen for focaccia and olive spread. Chef John Paul, a man of unwavering hostility, is, of course, yelling. His kitchen is a historical reenactment of a colonization that never took place; it's what would have happened if Colombia and Brazil had been conquered by a cursing Bostonian with a fabricated French accent. It's brown-skinned dishwashers, prep workers, and line cooks slaving for pitiful wages in a sweltering atmosphere of uninterrupted screaming.

John Paul says, "Hey, you got fuckin' Bruce Springsteen at table thirty-one?"

"Yeah, Chef."

"Is he a prick or what?"

"He seems okay."

"I knew it," he says. "A prick. Take good care of him, though. Don't fuck anything up."

"Wait," I say, "*don't* fuck anything up?"

"Don't get all cunty with me, Mary, just 'cause you're top of the list. Yeah, I saw that shit. Congratulations."

"Thanks, Chef. Especially for that 'cunty' part."

The list hangs at the bottom of the stairs behind a locked glass case. On a very basic level, it catalogs the servers in order of seniority and notes our schedule for the week. The first thing we do when we get to work is check the list. We can know exactly what our schedule is, but we look at the list to be sure things in the world are as they should be. I have been the most senior server in the restaurant for six days, ever since Cameron Lippy, drunk as always, fell out an open fourth-floor window and died.

Over these past three years, I've slowly climbed higher and higher, and now, thirty-five names below mine, it's an acknowledgement that I'm the best there is. It isn't the same as seeing your name on the cover of *Playbill*, but still, it makes me horny to look at it.

I love the feeling of being center stage, of everyone's eyes on me. Like most people from Freehold, I started out as a musician, writing songs and playing acoustic guitar, but I got sick of singing the same crappy songs over and over. Acting allowed me to play multiple roles. When you're good at it, you discover parts of yourself you never would have: pockets of compassion, of rage, of empathy for lives seemingly disconnected from your own. And you realize that Bruce Springsteen isn't a genius or a national hero; he's just a guy with a bit of talent who's gotten good at playing one appealing role. But say that in Jersey and some big-haired hootchie will bust a nail trying to rip out your tongue.

On the way to drop off focaccia, I pick up Shiny Head's wine. I set down the focaccia and olive spread at Bruce and Evan's table, tell them I'll be right back, and open and pour out the wine for the businessmen. Their appetizers are on the table.

"How is everything, gentlemen?" I ask.

"Great, Gabbi, thanks," they say, eyeing me like animals approaching a salt lick.

I go back to Bruce's table.

"I like this bread," Evan says. "Very tasty."

"You're Evan, right?"

"How did you know? Did you tell her, Dad?"

"I didn't tell her. Mary must know some things."

I just smile, say, "Can I answer questions about the menu? The steak au poivre is great. The tuna is excellent."

"I'm a vegetarian," Bruce says.

"You are?" I'm not sure why this is so shocking to me.

"For a few years now. I think I'll try your sweet potato ravioli."

Wouldn't news of this ruin his Everyman reputation as a champion of factory workers? I mean, who ever heard of a vegetarian rock star from New Jersey?

"I'll try the steak," Evan says. "Medium rare please."

I nod approvingly at him.

There's something I don't trust about vegetarians, with their PETA memberships and fake turkeys, their air of superiority. I have no doubt that when they're alone, it's nothing but bacon burgers, veal cutlets, and turducken.

At the server station, Bogan—who pokes his index finger in and out of his belly button when he's nervous—pokes away, and tells me that the restaurant was going to pick up Bruce's tab, but tables forty-five, seventy-one, and fifty-three want to buy him a round of drinks, four more tables have tried to order dessert for him, and Crazy Jack (self-named) wants to send him a bottle of Cristal *and* pick up his tab.

Crazy Jack is a lunatic drunk who recently sold his software company for a hundred million dollars. He tips the bar over a thousand dollars a night, crumpling hundred-dollar bills and throwing them into trash cans for the bartenders to dig out. I've never waited on him because he only requests the three or four servers who kiss his ass (and fuck him, if you believe the rumors) with the most gusto.

Bogan, knuckle-deep in belly button, says, "I suppose it's your table, though ultimately it's my call, but what, hypothetically, would you suggest we do, assuming you had the power to decide, which you don't?"

"Tell the other tables his tab is already taken care of and give the bill to Crazy Jack."

Bogan nods his head over and over as though this were the best idea he's ever heard and, still nodding, walks down the stairs, probably off to his office, where he's stashed all sorts of bottles that nobody is supposed to know about.

I scan the bar, find Crazy Jack with three snifters of vodka lined up in front of him, the nine olives the only thing he'll eat tonight. It's illegal in Massachusetts to pour someone a double, but for Jack, anything. On the rare occasions that he leaves the bar and heads into the dining room, it's like a storm blowing through. Servers have gotten into fistfights over the privilege of having Crazy Jack at their table.

Bruce and Evan eat their free appetizers in the midst of their own storm. Evan hasn't stopped talking since they sat down, and while Bruce must be aware of the bidding war his presence is causing, he concentrates on his son. Poor Evan probably has no idea of the pressure he'll someday feel to walk into a restaurant and cause a bidding war of his own. To grow up under Bruce Springsteen is to live uncomfortably within your own limits. I'll bet everyone in New Jersey, and especially Freehold, is given the hope that Springsteen's success offers, but without the talent and luck, what could be crueler?

From the coffee station, I watch Will and Kelvin at the service bar drinking deeply from paper cups. The coffee boy, a lanky seventeen-year-old named Timmy, has his own paper cup. One could almost believe it's his usual coffee with fourteen sugars, were it not for the fact, that, shirt untucked and wearing a cloudy grin, he's sculpting obscene animals out of wet espresso grounds and cinnamon sticks. What the hell is Marco thinking, giving alcohol to little private school Timmy who hopes to go to a Catholic college and study history? Shannon's sitting at the bar sharing a drink with the drunkest sorority member, a tiny thing with a great mouthful of white teeth. One of Shannon's tables is waving his check presenter in the air, hoping someone will take his money.

Bogan, returning up the stairs from his office, trips on the top step. I help him up, pick a scrap of trash from his hair, and get a vodka-infused *thanks* in return.

My God. The servers with their childish paper cups, the dark-skinned bussers doing all the work for our beautiful, affluent customers, who are themselves just barely keeping it together. *It isn't always like this*, I want to tell Bruce Springsteen. We aren't perfect, but tonight it seems that everyone has completely given up.

I don't think Bruce notices anything. His table is in the corner, a bit isolated from the main section of the restaurant, and, besides, he's probably used to ignoring his surroundings in public. A few customers approach his table and shake his hand. Servers bring him free drinks sent by their tables. Just look at the two Springsteens: feasting as though they were royalty. It's so like him to take over the only place I have any power.

I feel Mother's big hands on my shoulders. Together, we watch people swirl wine and spill coffee and blow on soup.

Will and Kelvin leave the service bar and drift toward us, probably coming for espressos to counter their vodka. Kelvin asks how my night's going, but before I can answer, he says, "Yeah. Speaking of masturbating truckers, last year alone jackknifed trucking accidents caused almost a billion dollars in damages and insurance increases."

Kelvin has a PhD in international finance from Harvard, and for the past nine months has been stalled midway through the first chapter of a book chronicling the economic implications of masturbating truckers. He continues, "They always claim that a car cut them off, but I guarantee it's no coincidence that truckers refer to jackknifing as 'jacking.'" He's completely sincere.

He does the universal gesture for masturbation, but it goes on for far too long and he's far too into it. I tell him to die. Slurring, Will asks me if Bruce and I have a date later. I tell him to die. Mother asks if I need a hug and I take it. Bogan appears and asks us if we think cavorting in front of guests is a sound business move.

I walk away, and when I'm sure he can't hear, I tell him to die.

My nine businessmen watch me with a mixture of lust, awe, and mockery as I balance and stack all their dishes along the length of my left arm. "Very impressive, Gabbi!" they say. Worse, however, than their looks and false praise, is the fact that I too am impressed by my plate-stacking ability.

I dump their dishes in the bus bucket, crumb their table, and set down dessert and after-dinner drink menus.

I check on Bruce's table, where their dinners have just been dropped off, and am told that everything is wonderful.

Shiny Head calls me over and stares at my breasts. "We'll take nine of them," he says.

"Two's not enough?" I don't even bother with the Italian accent, and he doesn't bother to notice.

"Cognacs," he says, pointing to the menu. "Nine cognacs," but he continues to stare.

There isn't a waitress alive who would punch a man with an $850 tab. Servers always joke about whoring ourselves—how the only difference between us and a prostitute is the penetration. We flirt and show skin and, if the tab is big enough, allow our asses to be patted and our tits accidentally brushed up against. So now, with this glistening-headed fuck staring at me, I know that not-punching is part of the performance, the only performing I'm doing these days, so I might as well make it good.

Bogan says to send Bruce three desserts, but he can barely get the words out. I've never seen him this wrecked so many hours before closing. "And coffees," he says. "Send that fucking kid an espresso, something to wipe off his goddamned smirk—Jesus, I hate kids!"

I nod encouragingly, then order Bruce a coffee and Evan a hot chocolate. The businessmen have another round of cognacs, leer some more, and eventually Shiny Head hands me a company credit card.

Normally, I wouldn't scam on such a large bill, but tonight I feel like I'm owed something. I'm not sure if it's this particular table or all the tables from all the preceding years, but somebody owes me something.

He tips twenty-five percent, and on top of the twenty percent I already added, I make four hundred dollars on the table.

Bruce is watching me, so I go over.

"We'll take a check whenever you can," he says.

"Desserts have been ordered for you. On the house."

"We're sort of in a hurry," Bruce says.

"What kind of desserts?" Evan asks.

And though it annoys me to have to sell the fact that we're giving him free desserts, I say, "Our three best: chocolate bread pudding, banana éclairs in hazelnut caramel sauce, and coconut sorbet over brandy-poached pears."

"We have a little extra time, don't we Dad?"

And what can he really say to that?

"And as for your bill," I say, "there's a line of people waiting to pay it. That guy over there"—I point to Crazy Jack, who's clutching his head in both hands and knocking over beer bottles with his chin—"eventually won the honors."

Bruce tries to act surprised, but he's a terrible actor. I can see that this happens to him everywhere he goes.

"Well," he says, nodding at Jack with affection, "that's very nice of him."

Bruce isn't exactly insincere, but he's clearly said the words so many times that they no longer have any meaning. Poor guy: he's probably just trying to teach Evan something about graciousness, but the years of fame have worn away his own capacity for it. He looks so old and awkwardly dressed. How strange that this is the man who has a fire truck dedicated to him in Freehold, "Born to Run" painted across its side.

I blurt, "I went to grad school at BU—I'm an actress— but I'm originally from Freehold. I used to eat pizza at Federici's, and breakfast at Sweet Lew's. I've heard those are your favorite places too."

We talk about Freehold, how it's getting so much bigger, nicer, and how each of us liked it better before all the bigness and niceness, and Evan says Freehold is the greatest place in the world. I think, *Yeah, if your father is Bruce Springsteen. If not, it's depressing and worthy of escape.* It's an annoying conversation; I don't care about all that's been torn down in Freehold and all that's recently gone up. And I'm angry that in talking about Freehold I feel such a fondness for it.

I interrupt him: "I was named after the Mary from 'Thunder Road.' When I hear your music in my parents' bedroom, I know not to disturb them. You and I have the same birthday."

As soon as I say it, I feel as though our similarities are something I've stolen from him—an act that requires forgiveness.

"That's really something," he says.

"Yeah," I say. "It's something."

"So what's an actress doing in Boston?"

"What?"

I can feel my heartbeat quicken. Was that some sort of snub?

"Why Boston," he continues, "and not New York or LA?"

"I don't know," I say, louder and more bitchy sounding than I would have liked. I pretend one of my other tables needs me.

I print out Bruce's check and head over to Crazy Jack. What the fuck kind of a question was that: *What's an actress doing in Boston?* How dare he judge me! He writes pop songs for people who believe in impossible escapes. And the worst thing is that I bought into it; what could be more improbable than making a living as an actress?

I put Bruce's check in front of Crazy Jack. He stares at it as though it were a particularly difficult riddle. I tell him it's Springsteen's. He looks at my breasts, and then my hips, and then my breasts, and, finally, my face.

"You take good care of him?" he says.

I force a smile.

He pulls out a softball-size mound of cash and peels off a large chunk, which he stuffs into the check presenter, smashing it as flat as it'll go. He strokes my hip, pulls me toward him, and kisses my ear.

Downstairs, I lock myself in the disgusting staff bathroom. If you're at the top of the list, people don't want to see you open a check presenter with hundreds of dollars in it. Also, you don't tip out the bussers, food runners, or bartenders on your scams, or on the drunken generosity of Crazy Jack, so it's none of their business how much is inside.

I pull apart the bills and count over six hundred dollars. The check, minus the free apps and desserts, came to sixty bucks. I'll make over nine hundred dollars tonight, almost three times what I've ever made.

I look in the mirror and try to see what Bruce Springsteen must see. *You met God today*, I think. The thought makes me laugh out loud, but, like Bruce's feigned surprise, the laughter is unconvincing. It's the feeling that though I met God, all he could offer me was nine hundred dollars.

At the dessert station, the pastry chef, a bearded, monk-like man, is deep in the weeds—dessert orders piled up in a precarious stack. He calmly dots a plate with caramel as though the precision of these dots is a matter of grave import. Upstairs, someone has turned the dining room music up way too loud. It's a Bruce Springsteen song, I realize, "Born in the USA," not one of my favorites.

"How long for the desserts on table thirty-one?" I ask.

He sets down his caramel, slowly reads through the stack of orders.

"I'm going to say fifteen minutes."

"Fifteen minutes! They're for Bruce Springsteen."

He looks at me, then returns to the orders, thumbs through them. "I respect his vegetarianism," he says. "How does twelve minutes strike you?"

I want to scream and knock that serenity off his face, but I've spent a long time training myself to either enhance or suppress emotions. I think of what Tom Stoppard said: *Actors are the opposite of people*, and I give him a smile totally lacking in impatience or humanity.

Will approaches, grabs a couple of desserts that look as though they've been waiting for quite a while. "So do you?" he says. "You two have a date?" His face is flushed and soggy.

"What are you talking about?"

"Bruce Springsteen. Are you two going to a drive-in together?"

"Why are you acting like this?"

"For your information, Cameron Lippy is dead. A few of us—not you!—have been toasting to a beautiful life that was cut way too short."

"You hated Cameron."

"That's just so fucked up! Maybe he was no 'Bruce Springsteen,' but he was my friend."

"You need another mint," I say, and give him two.

He throws them toward the trash—tells me that I make him so sick he could spit, and then he does, half on the floor, half on his shoe.

The pastry chef says, "Can you explain what's happening up there tonight?"

I shake my head. I don't have a clue.

The Springsteen music is absurdly loud. We always turn up the music as the night goes on, but this is ridiculous. The customers yell to hear each other above it. Evan proudly sings along, but Bruce looks embarrassed, as though he's unsure whether this is praise or mockery. He feels, I can tell, as though he's forcing this music on the rest of us, as though he were the one who requested we turn it up.

He's looking around for me.

Will, at the server station, is staring down Bruce Springsteen. He's pushing out his chest and seems to be getting worked up. Luckily, the station's twenty feet away, so Bruce is oblivious.

Bruce's eyes dart back and forth, his music blaring. He wants out.

I go to Will. "What are you doing?"

"I love you, Mary."

"No you don't. You're drunk."

"Fuck that! I love the shit out of you and you treat me like a joke." He actually has tears in his eyes, which makes me tear up. It's suddenly very obvious that he does, in fact, love me, and that I've been ignoring all the signs. I feel like I'm about to crumble, though I have no idea why.

Will leans in to kiss me, and I flee.

Bruce catches my eye and waves me over.

"Mary," he yells above the music, "are those desserts coming, or . . ."

"I'm really sorry about the wait," I yell back. "They'll be up in about ten minutes."

"Ten . . . Jesus Christ!" He flops back in his chair dramatically. "We're really in a hurry."

"All we're doing is going back to the hotel," Evan says to his father.

"Evan," he says, "just be quiet, okay?"

"Mr. Springsteen," I say, "everyone is having to wait. Your *free* desserts will be right out."

Behind me, above all of the noise, I can make out the sound of Will screaming obscenities.

"Is that waiter talking to me?" Bruce asks. He points to Will, still twenty feet away, who's staring at us and shouting. And it does seem he's yelling at Bruce Springsteen, something about how the Boss can't fuck any woman he wants just because he's the Boss. It's really hard to hear him, however, so maybe I'm mistaken.

I step closer to Bruce Springsteen so that we're just a foot apart. I put on my Samantha face, a character I play with aggressive customers. I say, "Why would he be yelling at you? You're revered. You're the most exciting thing that has ever happened to this restaurant."

"You ass-licking fuckwad!" Will screams. "You ain't my boss, Boss! Not mine!"

"Clearly he's yelling at someone."

"Not you, that's for certain."

Then I switch roles, from Samantha the brawny waitress who won't be pushed around to Carmen Pillipin, the cocky district attorney I played in BU's production of *Passing the Bar*. I say, "Evan, you don't think he's yelling at your father, do you?"

Carmen's leading question works like a Jedi trick: "Definitely not," he agrees. "He's yelling at someone else."

I take it one step further: "In fact," I say to Bruce, "I don't think he's yelling at anyone. It's loud in here. We're celebrating your music. He isn't yelling."

"He isn't yelling?" Bruce asks.

Behind me, Will's continued assault—the Boss is a shit eater, a biscuit snatcher, a ball chewer. Bogan lurches by with a look of impending violence.

"Of course not," I continue, and it feels as though, with each word, I'm growing stronger and he's shrinking. I switch to Momma Peters, an old role: "Nobody is yelling darlin'; we're so honored to have you here; you won't believe the magnificence of our chocolate bread pudding; we're all doing the best we can."

He looks baffled, yet nonetheless convinced.

And all at once, the old, buried sensations flood in—of standing ovations, of knowing that an audience is hanging on my every gesture; the almost forgotten feeling of being exceptional at something I care terribly for. Boston? What kind of a person pursues acting in Boston?

Bruce smiles, leans back in his chair, and waits for the magnificent desserts. He bobs his head to the loud, catchy music.

MARYVILLE,
CALIFORNIA, POP. 7

MARYVILLE IS A city of seven people: four houses hidden by a dense shield of trees and brush. All I hear from my front porch is our neighbor's daughter, Delia, playing hopscotch, the buzz of insects, the gentle breaking of waves.

We receive no phone bills or cable bills, although all of us have phones and our televisions get hundreds of channels. For mail, we ride a bike ten minutes down Pacific Coast Highway to a post office box in Huntington Beach. When we turn on the faucet, water comes out—*Take as many hot showers as you like*, says Jackson, our landlord and the founder of Maryville. *There's all the hot water in the world here*. Flip a switch and the lights come on, but we never see bills for this, either. Somehow, Maryville has managed to slip between the cracks.

Courtney tells me to enjoy the place and not worry about cracks. She and I have been together three years, mostly traveling from one beach city to the next. She's twenty-nine, two years older than me, and she fixes things, all things: people's neuroses and squeaky doors, shaken relationships and leaky birdbaths.

Courtney and I were in Costa Rica when I got my dad's letter. *Your mother*, he wrote. *It's spread to her bones*. He mentioned his own cancer in the P.S.

We headed back through Nicaragua and Guatemala in my old Toyota, not stopping for anything. I kept thinking about how my mother was in labor with me for fifty-two hours. My parents would remind me of those fifty-two painful hours whenever they could, using it as a way to get me to take out garbage cans or to stop crying about being dropped off at Grandma's while they took one of their trips. I fell for it every time.

She probably died while we were driving through Baja. By the time we made it home, my father couldn't speak—from the cancer or from losing her, I don't know. We stayed with him for four weeks, then a week in the hospital. Then he was gone.

We had one funeral reception for both of them. Two hundred people crammed into their old house, half of whom I'd never before seen. Each of them had stories: my parents, back to back, throwing punches in a bar fight they'd started, of them being scolded by an Italian priest for skinny-dipping in a baptismal pool; a Greek couple who'd flown in for the funeral told an unsettling story about the care with which my mother had removed a small branch from my father's anus after they'd made love in an olive orchard in Santorini. I was hearing about a life of which I knew nothing.

Everyone kept drinking, kept hugging me, and though Courtney wanted us to stay, I felt like a stranger among these people. We squeezed into the tiny bed in my old room, listening to the sounds of toasting glasses and laughing downstairs. It was just like when I was a kid.

Courtney drove us away the next day. The absence of my parents felt like drowning, which I had never feared in fifteen years of surfing. I just couldn't catch my breath.

My dad often told stories about Mom's screams during my birth—how they echoed through the hospital corridors with such violence that they forced the rest of the pregnant mothers to reconsider. If he'd been drinking, the screams even shattered a few hospital windows. I came to love these stories because they were about me. There's no way I could remember those screams, but on that drive I did—could even hear the sounds my father made trying to soothe her. I struggled to focus on Courtney, who didn't stop speaking. I don't know what she was saying, but the sound of her voice was a life jacket.

Courtney was the one who found Maryville. Out of nowhere, she swerved off Pacific Coast Highway toward a grove of trees. I grabbed on to the dashboard for support.

"There's a path," she said. "I want to follow it."

"What path!"

"Just calm down."

I let go of the dashboard, and yes, it did seem we were on a path, or at least a break in the brush with just enough room for our truck to squeeze through. We drove on this dirt road for about a hundred feet until we reached a large clearing. Four simple one-story houses traced the outskirts of the clearing. In the center was a wooden sign. We thought it was a joke: *Maryville, California, Pop. 5.* That was four months ago.

Each morning we wake up long before the sun rises. I brew coffee and put out cream and sugar while Courtney stirs butter, bananas, peanuts, and shredded coconut into simmering oatmeal. We need caffeine and fat to fuel the hours of surfing.

We eat on the porch, watching old Elizabeth knit scarves—what does she do with all of them! She has long, wispy white hair and smooth pink skin, like a Swedish child, or a good witch. She'll stop her knitting long enough to wave to us, but then she's right back at it. Everyone's usually asleep at Darryl and Kendra's, but Jackson is always awake. Most days we invite him over from his porch to ours, and when he comes, he'll bring a bag of mangoes or an apple crisp still warm from the oven. We pay him two hundred dollars a month in rent, but sometimes he tells us to forget the money, that what he really wants is one of Courtney's home-cooked meals. He shows up to these free-rent dinners with two dozen roses and champagne and a chocolate cake far too big to ever finish. He'll tell dream-like stories about Mary, his late wife, after whom Maryville was named.

"For a month straight, we made love on the roofs of igloos," he told us on the first of these dinners. We were sitting on our porch attacking his cake with forks. "She'd howl," he continued, "and it would attract polar bears and snow leopards, so I'd put my forearm in her mouth to quiet her down."

If a lightbulb blows, Jackson will appear at the door with a new one. Once, when I cut my hand chopping garlic, he walked in with a Band-Aid before Courtney even got back from the bathroom to tell me we were out of them. Maryville is Jackson's.

Afternoons, I paint at the empty beach closest to Maryville. It's a one-minute walk over our sand-and-dirt clearing, through the trees that hide us, and across Pacific Coast Highway. Our first week here, in the days when I'd set my director's chair in the living room while Courtney put up photos or plugged in the phone—when I silently watched her set up our life—we talked about this being our own private surfing beach. There's no easy way to get here; you have to climb a six-foot fence. Nowhere to park, no snack stands, bathrooms, or Boogie Board rentals. "Your very own ocean," Courtney told me. The waves, however, are small and unsurfable, so it's where I paint instead. In any beach city in the world, I can make a living selling pictures of the ocean to tourists whose lives have planted them in a dry spot.

I paint the ocean exactly as it is, because every day it's different. It's the same, too, of course. Water moves the way water moves—the predictable cycle of the tides, chartable depths, the consistent arc of waves. Courtney was raised on Cape Cod, amid that comforting rhythm, which might explain her optimism. I'm from Phoenix, but have lived near oceans and near Courtney long enough to know that mourning and even grieving are just part of the cycle, temporary as low tide. Nevertheless, this knowledge feels about as comforting as if a shark, between bites of my leg, assured me that he'd be finished soon enough.

This afternoon, an oil tanker appears at the horizon like the onset of a headache. It's easily a hundred yards long, the biggest object I've ever seen, red on the bottom and black on top, like some exotic, deadly insect. The closer it chugs toward the beach and into my painting, the more I feel it won't ever stop—that it'll come crashing ashore and smash through Maryville. Which is stupid. Of course it stops, about three hundred yards from shore, its gleaming black top undulating in the sun as though it were a mirage. I try to paint around it, but it spans my entire line of vision. So I leave, embarrassed to have an oil tanker chase me off, and then more embarrassed when, as always, I get lost going home.

Walking or riding my bike, day or night, I often miss the path off PCH and have to backtrack, passing it again and again until, by dumb luck, I finally stumble across it. For a while I tried leaving markers at the head of the path—a crushed bar of surf wax, a banana peel—but they were always gone by the time I got back. I asked Courtney if the path had ever eluded her in this way, and she stared at me for a bit before saying, "Of course it does. I mean, there's that pesky spatial vortex, right?"

She's just trying to demystify this place, help me to get grounded, but you know what? Fuck her. The path disappears. The place doesn't want to be found.

The tanker is still there the next morning as we bike to the beach. I ask, "Have you seen that?" Courtney skids to a stop.

She stares at it, as though trying to come to some deep understanding. I watch her and wait. She's six feet tall, just an inch shorter than me, the only tall girlfriend I've ever had. Her hair is long and bleached blond by the sun, her skin deep brown and freckled. I can't tell if it's just her height, but she's more substantial than other people.

"I'll bet you a fiver I can hit it," she finally says, setting down her board, and then picking up and launching a rock. It doesn't even make it to the water.

She scowls. Gets back on her bike. "Come on," she says, "the sun is about to rise."

The secret is to avoid people.

We have to get there before the meatheads in wet suits—the hungover assholes who brag about the pussy they're getting or want to get, the buff kids who snake Courtney's waves and don't understand a thing about surfing.

Surfing is this: being pushed over a ten-foot waterfall and finding, suddenly, that you've been given the gift of flight.

The best waves, however, are near the Huntington Beach pier, so the only way to avoid the people we need to avoid is to get there while they're asleep. The sexy people parading down Main Street with their bleached hair and fake boobs just confirm all the stereotypes about southern California. It isn't healthy to see them. We avoid the mothers with porn-star bodies and smooth, ageless skin. My mother was wrinkled, pale, perfectly average really, but dumpy by today's standards. She went gray in her late thirties, and during the summer she'd wear shorts and bikini tops: cellulite on her thighs, stretch marks on her belly. Supposedly she couldn't talk for three days following my delivery. I imagine these California mothers unconscious with drugs, the baby, clean and diapered, gently plucked from their perfect bodies.

It's important to avoid their children as well—flawless, too-healthy kids who never seem to frown or throw tantrums. It's as though southern California were breeding a new race of super-beautiful people. A race, by the way, that scares me. Next to these kids—never sad, never cold, never sick a day in their lives—I feel diseased. There's no space here for sadness. You can get angry and people will understand, but sadness is a foreign language.

So I get angry. *Fifty-two hours of screaming?* I just can't see it. She wasn't one of those mothers who had grilled cheese ready when her kid got home from school. She had flocks of friends. She had her job at the real estate agency—just a part-time bookkeeper, but she took it seriously. She had my father, their date-nights, their long mornings alone, their trips. At the first sign of pain she would have instructed them to knock her out with morphine until it was over. I think he only told the goddamned story so often because he was angry I'd hurt her.

The ocean is warm and I can see my feet floating beneath me in the murky way a shark must see. It's May; I haven't felt a cold wind in two months and there's a long summer coming. I watch Courtney surf—the way she works even the smallest wave to get everything she can out of it, but also how she lacks grace. She's always a step behind the wave, lanky, slow, and stiff. She sure doesn't surf like someone who grew up near an ocean, and that clumsiness gives me more satisfaction than it should.

Closer to shore, I see Jackson and Delia—his enormous long-board ridiculous next to Delia's four-footer. She's only seven, but Jackson convinced her parents, Kendra and Darryl, that the sooner they put her in the ocean, the better off she'd be. He's careful with her, never strays more than a few feet away, but I still wonder where he gets such faith that nothing will happen. Again and again, the whitewash surges past her, the board moves forward and she falls off before getting close to standing. And then she's under, waves rolling over top, rocks on the ocean floor, stingrays, riptides. She could hit her head on the edge of her board. She always pops back up, but how can he know that one day she won't just disappear?

When I was an infant, my mother and father took me to the water ballet classes they took at the community pool. I've begun to remember this time, the sharp smell of chlorine, the blaring orchestral music, floating lightly through the water with their huge hands beneath me. Courtney refers to these memories as "delusions." My sadness is starting to annoy her. What she would do is cry for a couple of weeks, mourn her loss, and then remember the best things about them. She wouldn't start doubting the tale of her birth or conjuring memories she couldn't possibly possess. But I'm not deluded, I'm remembering, and the pool's water is as real as the ocean beneath me now.

That night, I lie awake thinking of oil tankers. Courtney is beside me, snoring softly. She's an amazing sleeper—falls asleep as soon as her head hits the pillow, never has nightmares, wakes for nothing. I've surfed at beaches all over the world—must have seen hundreds of oil tankers, but I never really noticed any of them. They were just another part of the ocean, as expected as the seaweed or the fear of lurking sharks. But here I am, awake.

And I can hear the tanker. Beyond Courtney's steady breathing, insects outside, the ocean breaking against the shore, is a deep rumbling—a bassy, guttural growl, like an animal warning you to back off. Because of it I can't sleep. So I get up.

Though it's the middle of the night, Jackson is on his porch and he waves me over. "Can't sleep, son?" he says.

He's on a rocking chair drinking whiskey from a tall glass filled with ice, and I sit in the other rocking chair. I say, "There's a tanker out there and I think I hear it." I point into the blackness toward the ocean.

"I don't hear it," he says, "but I guess that don't mean it's not there."

We rock in our chairs, Jackson sipping from his drink. I listen to the groans of the tanker in conversation with his ice clinking against glass. Four months in Maryville. One hundred twenty-two days of the same routines, same sadness, same cloudless skies. This tanker and the noise it's brought will be the first change.

"I've started writing down Delia's sentences," Jackson says, "in a little book I have. Today she said, 'Light is made out of blindness.' She's gonna get up on that board. You'll see."

"Be standing any day now," I say, even though I doubt she will.

"Delia would have loved Mary," he muses. "Kids we didn't even know would climb onto Mary's lap and hold her hand." He takes a long drink. "Ever tell you how I built Maryville?"

"No," I say.

I don't want to know. I know everything I need to know about Maryville—that our home was vacant because it was waiting for us, that Jackson would never raise our rent, that we're so hidden here that nobody knows we exist.

"This was so long ago you wouldn't believe me if I told you."

He starts to tell his story, but the tanker seems so loud. I hear Jackson, as though from a great distance, saying that the ocean used to cover this land, that the sun was hotter then, and the sand whiter and finer. And then he's talking about the scent of Mary's hair, like warm peaches. "I never even realized it was warm peaches until after she died. You learn things about people after they're gone."

"That's true," I say, realizing it is. I've learned that the only way my parents identified themselves was through their love for one another. They were parents, but didn't see themselves as such; they worked in boring offices doing tedious, unrewarding work, but they didn't see that either. They saw themselves as heroic lovers with an insatiable lust for both life and love. Of course they'd have to die together.

Before they died I couldn't have named a single flaw. It's probably just a way of dealing with death. I've found, however, that despite my newfound ability to identify their failings, I still can't get used to the world without them.

"Maryville was what I built with my grief," Jackson blurts out, as though he's just made this discovery.

I shrug my shoulders. I don't want to hear it. I keep my grief to myself and he can do the same.

He finishes the last of his drink and starts crunching ice. "Guess how Mary died," he says.

"What? No."

"Go on. I want you to."

"Jackson . . ."

"Just do it, okay. Just guess."

"Car accident," I say.

"Guess again."

"Heart attack? Drowned? Choked on a chicken bone? I don't know what you want me to say."

"Wrong, wrong, and wrong. She was bit by a bat, had a reaction to it, and died."

I wait for him to say more. The story seems so incomplete, and I almost give in to all of my questions. Questions like, *You've got to be fucking kidding me: a bat? When did the ocean cover Maryville? Why don't we get electricity bills? How long can any of this last?* But I don't want these questions answered. I don't want to hear that Jackson and this place claim some sort of mystical power, and I also don't want to hear that the secret to our free electricity is simply a spliced power line. I want neither the magic nor the rationalization explained. I rock back and forth, while the tanker rumbles.

"You really can't hear that?"

The next morning: Courtney making breakfast, the tanker silent. I watch her peel an overripe banana and think about rot. "Time is the enemy of beauty," I announce, aware that I sound like a C-grade philosopher. She thinks about this, eating her brown banana, a spoonful of peanut butter.

"What about aged beef?" she says. "And wine. Glacier-forged canyons? What about love? You're wrong; things get better with time." She picks up an apple from the counter, takes a bite, and walks onto the porch. And suddenly I can see us very clearly: two strangers trying hard to figure each other out. I can see, for example, that if Courtney ever left, this is how I'd remember her: walking barefoot onto the porch eating an unwashed apple.

Later, in my painting, the tanker has narrow eyes and teeth. There's a dark, foamy ocean and a full moon spotlighting a little girl digging in the sand. I imagine her digging blindly every day and night for a treasure, the contents of which she couldn't begin to name. I paint agony on her face, dark, slurred strokes, jagged, thick texture. No tourist will buy it.

Something is happening, beginning with windless, cloudless days, and full moons; late at night, at the beach where I paint, the tanker makes its noise, and the waves get huge—six to eight feet, breaking cleanly and barreling slowly along the coast, patiently like a pianist traveling the length of the keys. "It's the tanker," I say, but nobody hears me.

A month passes—a summer month, hot and still, except for the nights. Around midnight, the tanker calls out and the waves answer. And they're some of the best waves we've ever seen, so we begin sleeping during the day.

On one of these nights, Jackson paddles up to us, towing Delia on her little board. "You're up real late, Delia," Courtney says, paddling to her and kissing her wet head.

I'd been watching Delia fall all night, the full moon illuminating each failed attempt.

"I'm not even tired at all," she says.

"Can I ask something?" Jackson says. "You haven't told anyone about this, have you?"

"About what?" Courtney wonders, but I know what he's asking: about the waves, about the tanker, about Maryville.

"No," I say, "of course not."

"That's probably better. We're having a lot of luck here, and I'm not sure the whole damn world needs to know about it."

Delia says, "I saw luck swim right under my board."

"Yeah?" Courtney says. "Where was it going?"

"Away from here, that's for sure."

Figures, I think, but I don't say anything.

When Jackson and Delia paddle to shore, I say, "Delia's pretty weird."

"No, *Delia's* just imaginative. What's weird is you and Jackson, like a couple of little boys afraid someone will discover your secret fort."

"Right," I say, "and what if those assholes from the pier started coming here?"

"So fearful," she continues, "like you and the tanker."

"I hate that tanker," I say, and having said it, realize how much I mean it.

"Let's paddle out to it," she says. "Maybe the two of you could come to an understanding."

"It's much further than it looks." I tell her about the cold, and the sharks, the terrible riptides. "We could never make it that far out. Never."

She touches my face and says, quietly, "Okay, love. Okay."

Jackson decides that July's rent would be better paid by a free-rent dinner, so Courtney goes all out: avocado soup topped with watermelon pieces, baked brie filled with homemade apricot chutney, sautéed spinach and sun-dried tomatoes (both from her garden), truffle mashed potatoes, and, of course, Jackson's favorite, sesame seared salmon. She has me etch ocean scenes into the sourdough rolls before baking. Normally, it's just the three of us at these meals, but tonight Courtney's invited Elizabeth, the old lady who knits.

Jackson shows up with pies, a stack of them: apple, a chocolate peanut butter, strawberry banana cream. He brings a case of beer and a bottle of Scotch. I take the pies from his arms, and Courtney makes room in the refrigerator for all that beer. "There's four of us," I say. "You think just the three pies will be enough?"

"I wasn't sure what everyone liked," he says.

"Don't listen to him, Jackson. You're a very generous man and we appreciate you." She kisses him, and he tells her she's an angel. People are often telling Courtney she's an angel.

"You said four people," Jackson says to me. "Who's the fourth?"

"I invited Elizabeth," Courtney explains.

"Oh you did, did you?" and they exchange a look.

Elizabeth brings ice cream she churned herself— hazelnut, my favorite—but I find myself disappointed she hasn't brought us a scarf. She's devoted her life to them, and I guess I wanted to see one up close.

Watching Elizabeth eat, I realize why she's always seemed familiar. She's left-handed, like my mother, and watching her spread brie onto a cracker with her left hand, my eyes tear up.

I look at Jackson and Elizabeth, thinking Courtney probably told them about my parents, knowing I wouldn't want her to. I know where Courtney and I were when my mom died. We weren't just somewhere in Baja. We were at a diner in Ensenada. We ordered and she was still alive. When our food came, she was dead. I just knew it. Courtney said, "Is something wrong? It looks good, right?" and she pointed to my plate of eggs, beans, and tortillas. What could I say?

It's a quiet meal, despite the two separate conversations: mine and Courtney's, and Jackson and Elizabeth's. My attempts fail to merge the two, and since nobody else seems to mind, I stop trying. I talk to Courtney and watch Elizabeth scoop up potatoes and shake pepper onto her fish.

"My mom was an awful cook," I say.

"The worst," Courtney agrees, "but your dad didn't seem to mind."

"I think he got too used to it." My roll has a picture of two dolphins leaping through a wave.

"Remember the linguini with bacon sauce?" she says.

"Oh my god, it was terrible."

"Or the sweet potato curry with Swiss cheese?"

"I remember. That curry was the worst thing anyone has ever made."

"You're missing them a lot," she says.

"I don't know."

"You are." Courtney often names what I'm feeling before I know what it is. I can't admit this to her, of course.

"Still," Courtney says, "I learned a lot from her experiments. Your mom was a wild, fearless cook."

I like the sound of that: *a wild, fearless cook*. Sometimes my memories are invocations capable of bringing them back, but other times they just sting. Tonight, my parents feel close.

Eventually, Courtney and I clear the dishes, brew coffee, and bring out the pies and ice cream. The way Elizabeth stirs her coffee, the peculiar left-handedness of it, I have to talk to her. I say the only thing I can think of: "Why do you knit all those scarves?"

"That's crocheting, honey."

"Crocheting, then. You always wear short sleeves, so why scarves?"

"Maybe she likes scarves," Courtney says.

"I only have about fifteen," she says. "I usually just take them apart."

"I don't understand," I say.

"Most of the time, they turn out adequate instead of exceptional, so I unweave them and start again."

"You do super work," Courtney says. "Doesn't she, Jackson?"

"She's wonderful."

"What's the difference, though?" I ask. "What makes one scarf average and one exceptional?"

"I'm not sure I could explain it. It isn't really a physical thing . . . mostly luck; I do all this work and sometimes I'm rewarded with a miracle . . . beyond my control, as though . . ." but I can't even hear her anymore, so engrossed am I in her gesturing, her left hand tracing arcs back and forth—moons and waves—and it's as though my mother were speaking to me, her words always less meaningful than the gestures that accompanied them, and I think I understand what Elizabeth's hands are saying: the shapelessness of perfection or imperfection, of being wounded or being healed, and the imperceptible way one becomes the other.

Later that night, Courtney and I make love, our bodies salty and dry from so much time in the ocean. Her eyes follow mine: from her nose to her ear, to the pillow, the wall—and it's uncomfortable, how I can't get away, so I close my eyes. When this is over, she'll rinse herself, and then I will, and we'll sleep through the morning, until the afternoon heat is too much. I'll paint another picture of the tanker, we'll cook something, and at midnight, under a full moon, we'll surf the perfect waves. Our skin, hot now, begins to stick together, all that salt. These days can't continue; this just isn't what a life looks like. If I open my eyes, she'll see me.

Two months of surfing in perfect conditions has brought us closer to the ocean than we've ever been. Finally, after all these years, the board feels like a natural extension of myself, as though I'd sprouted a new limb. It's the same with Courtney—she's caught up to the ocean, or it slowed down for her, but it's like she's found grace.

On this night, the full moon spotlights the tanker. Beside me, Courtney straddles her board, her long body blue in the moonlight. She says, "Do you think these waves can last?"

"The waves will last as long as the tanker's here."

In her silence it sounds preposterous, but still, I believe it. I say, "And have you noticed the moon has been full like every night?"

"No," she says, "it hasn't. The moon is just the moon."

"I'm not so sure." Miracles aren't as rare as people say. Sometimes they swarm, inescapable. And sometimes instead of granting a gift, they sever.

"Let me show you then," Courtney says, and before I can speak, she's paddling toward the tanker.

I call out, but she keeps going. So I climb up on my board and follow. I paddle and paddle, but I can't catch up, and the tanker keeps getting further away. My shoulders start to ache and my hands go numb. Still, I paddle.

The tanker grows huge, blotting out the moon entirely. Courtney waits just ahead, and when I get to her, she says, "Catch me," and she's gone, heading toward the biggest thing I've ever seen.

The weight of it sucks us in, and for a second it feels like we'll be crushed. The noise is deafening, just water crashing against water, but the great mass of the tanker amplifies everything. Courtney maneuvers forward, steadying herself with a palm against its side. She ties her leash to the bottom of a ladder and starts climbing up. Midway to the top she looks down at me like a little girl scampering up a tree. Dizzied, I turn away. Why should it be frightening just because it's big? Why can't I even look at it? The shore is a distant streak—a single light, which I imagine to be Jackson's porch light, though probably it isn't. From above, Courtney's voice: "Oh, my God!" she screams, laughing. "You've got to see this."

It's cold out here, dark in the enormous shadow of the tanker, the water black. There's a smell like boiled meat and tar. I imagine all the life swimming below me, and Courtney laughing above, but I can't figure out what to do. I paddle to the ladder, which looks sturdy enough. And it comes upon me all at once, the certainty that I'll never set foot on land again. That I'll never walk around Maryville or sleep in a bed. And then there's sharks swimming between my legs, their teeth scraping my heels, and this nauseating, intense need to flee. I try to breathe. I tell myself, *Don't leave her out here*. I reach for the ladder, thinking it might shock me, though it doesn't. It's cool and dense, and the heft of it helps with the sharks I understand to be phantoms. Still, knowing they're not real does nothing to dissolve the large shapes I see floating beneath me. I tie my leash beside Courtney's, grip tightly, and climb up.

The deck of the tanker is like a huge, empty playground. There are two lawn chairs bolted at the edge of the deck and Courtney is sitting on one of them. "The view," she says. "Like one of your paintings."

"Somebody could come," I whisper, though the deck is entirely flat and I don't see from where anyone would emerge. For some reason it's pleasant up here, like we're on a cruise ship.

I sit beside her and watch the ocean glowing in the moonlight—decide that the single glimmer in the distance actually is Jackson's porch light. Earlier in the night, we had a barbecue: me and Courtney, Darryl, Kendra, and Delia, Jackson and Elizabeth. Kendra and Elizabeth took turns holding Delia, who squealed each time Jackson read one of her sentences: *God knits the dead people an elegant tuxedo. If I had a treasure, I would dress it in silk and speak to it gently and sweetly.* I was thinking that I really liked these people, but that Delia was a bit nuts, and probably Kendra and Darryl were nuts, too, to let her surf in the middle of the night with their landlord. I was thinking that I respected Elizabeth's attempt at perfection, but *come on*, weaving and unweaving scarves every day?

I was thinking about Courtney, who kept nudging me and raising her eyebrows toward Elizabeth and Jackson. It amazes me the way she's always up to something, planting vegetables or setting people up. And she'll succeed, too— everything she plants grows—and then we'll be three couples and a child, still a strange town, but a little less lonely perhaps. Maybe the reason I can't find the path into Maryville isn't because the place is somehow protected from outsiders, but simply because I inherited my mother's awful sense of direction. The moonlight is so bright that I can make out two lone surfers three miles up the coast.

This morning Delia stood up on her board. She surfed. At the time, it seemed miraculous—not the fact that she was standing, but the way Jackson appeared to be orchestrating the whole thing. He stood behind her, raising his arms as though casting a spell, and as his arms rose, Delia rose as well. I can see now that he was just reaching out to catch her if she fell.

I close my eyes against the moonlight and feel Courtney's hand in mine. I think, *fifty-two hours*; the moon could have risen and set, risen and set. And I'm remembering something: my parents in a doctor's office being told she's pregnant with me. They both start crying at the same time, and then go right to comforting each other. *It won't be the end of our lives*, they say.

And then a chill, just a little thing, but I can tell that summer is ending. Though the changing of the seasons in southern California is so subtle it can barely be called a change, summer is special—its stillness and utter perfection. I say to Courtney, "We'll have to start wearing our wet suits soon."

"Tell me what you're really thinking," she says.

"I'm missing them a lot."

"I know," she says, "but I'm here."

I turn away from the moon, from the ocean, from the light in Jackson's house. I lean in and her arms cover me. It feels like falling, how far I sink into her.

NAUTICAL INTERVENTION

> *To lift man in air*
> *and strangle strangle strangle*
> *not so fun as seems*
> —BERTOK MELLES

the *pertunda*

A thirty-seven-foot schooner heading south under power at twelve knots in the Ionian Sea, northwest of Corfu.

Pertunda: Roman goddess of sexual love and pleasure, presides over the marriage bed. That is, the deflowering of virgins.

the main deck

Cap gives the signal to cut the boat's engine, so Little John cuts the engine.

Bertok, who gets an itch in the middle of his back when-ever he's nervous and who's entirely too muscle bound to get near the itch, tries to scratch it with the tip of his machete.

Cap gives me the *help Bertok out, he's liable to butcher him-self with that machete* look, so I scratch the itch. Bertok moans lightly, remembers the command for silence was given ten minutes ago, and tries to blend the moan into something aquatic, a porpoise call is my guess. Cap gives him an approving nod.

Little John steers us toward the yacht. Daeng pulls his balaclava tight and passionately strokes the shaft of his AK-47. His glass eye shimmers in the Mediterranean night sky: He enjoys this way too much.

The yacht we are approaching, the *Good Life*, is dark; they're asleep, whoever they are. It's what people mean by clockwork, I suppose, the way we all know our parts. Bertok hooks the steel ladder to their starboard bow and Daeng slings back his automatic and goes first, his little frame scampering like a woolly bug.

Once aboard, he does a series of Hollywood somer-saults and backflips, producing a pair of Colt 45s that he points in all directions. My weapon of choice is a solid birch rolling pin, an agile yet not too deadly companion who's gotten me out of some hairy situations in addition to rolling out delicate, buttery piecrusts. Daeng does his seagull call, which means *all clear* and Cap, Bertok, and I climb aboard. Little John waits with the boat. He's too good-hearted and utterly not fearsome. Also, his *the patrol boat is coming* hoot is a perfect mimic of a sperm whale song. It's uncanny.

Below deck, we split into two groups. I'm stuck with Daeng, who keeps asking, "Time?" and then answering it himself: "Ninety seconds!" "A hundred twenty seconds!" At the bedroom door, he pauses and gives me an elaborate sequence of hand signals. They could mean anything, but I think they say, *I'll riddle them with bullets and you thrash the corpses with your rolling pin.* I respond with my high school baseball coach's signs: *steal second base, slide, the suicide squeeze.*

He shakes his head at my lack of professional brutality, kicks down the door and does another of those somersaults into the room. I step over the discarded door, annoyed that it was probably unlocked anyway, but as Cap is always reminding us, it's chiefly Daeng's showmanship that makes him a successful pirate.

I flip a light switch and Daeng shouts, "Who wants to fucking die?"

The middle-aged couple in the enormous canopy bed look a lot like I'd look if I were woken up by a hairy Indonesian maniac in a black mask pointing an AK-47 at me and asking if I wanted to die.

"Nobody's going to die," I say, pointing to my rolling pin.

"No way," he says. "Last time nobody died and it was bullshit!"

"Nobody dies."

He raises a bushy eyebrow and pumps his hips toward the woman.

"No," I say. "Absolutely not."

We march them onto the main deck where Bertok is duct-taping the hands and feet of two men and two women, all of them tan, gray-haired, and sporting crisp silk pajamas. Bertok is a virtuoso with duct tape and a machete and it's a shame they're too afraid to enjoy his handiwork. When all six are bound, Cap steps forward.

the spiel

"Ladies and gentlemen, I'm Captain Arthur Trilling." He walks behind them and shakes their bound hands. Cap is decked out in his usual working attire: black linen pants, black leather sandals, a royal blue button-down shirt, and a burgundy ascot. His jet-black hair is peppered with white, as is his perfectly trimmed beard. He's an immaculate guy: gives himself manicures, pedicures, under-eye treatments, salt scrubs. He sighs mournfully to illustrate the weight of his coming speech.

"Piracy," he begins.

He gives the whole spiel. It's important to Cap that people understand the historical context behind us stealing all their stuff—that, for instance, simply by owning a yacht, they're challenging the underprivileged to just try and take away their wealth. Cap's grandfather was an actor who achieved some measure of fame as a pirate in the silent films, and his father ran a Caribbean-themed eatery in Pasadena. Cap's great-grandfather, however, was the real deal: a pirate who successfully plagued four of the seven seas.

As always, Cap brings up Blackbeard, his idol. He talks about how Blackbeard's biggest weapon was the ability to cause fear: how he'd stick slow-burning matches among his whiskers and behind his ears in order to appear ablaze with power.

"Fear," Cap explains, "is far stronger than all the muscles on this man here." He points to Bertok, who shrugs, clearly not in agreement.

"I'd wreck Blackbeard," Bertok says. "Everybody know that." The six, bound and lined up as though awaiting execution, try to smile encouragingly.

Cap is interested in timelessness. His greatest pleasure comes from imagining the time, well after his death, when people will speak of him with the sort of reverence associated with other genius-villains, such as Blackbeard or Billy the Kid. He believes in a perfect act of piracy, a flawless performance in which the five of us and our "customers" (Cap's word) would know exactly where to move and what to say, in which there'd be a progressive sense of movement, the entire experience adding up to more than the sum of its parts (in the same way the five of us together are greater than any of us could have been on our own).

He thinks he's helping people: the terror they're subjected to will ultimately aid them in reassessing the value of their lives. In the perfect heist, they'd have this epiphany while the heist was happening.

While Cap's in instructional mode and Daeng is off with his burlap sack collecting the goodies, I head to the galley. I'm pleased to discover that somebody aboard this boat fancies himself a chef. Obviously whoever it is, is a hack; I can tell by their knives—Sabatier, so ridiculously overpriced— also they have mild olive oil and store-bought curry powder. There are, however, some indications of decency: eight tins of Sevruga caviar, a huge cut of perfectly marbled tenderloin, three bottles of cognac, a spice grinder, two cases of adequate burgundy, some black truffle oil, and a nice-sized hunk of fresh ricotta salata.

I hump the supplies back on deck where Daeng is waiting and Cap is finishing up. "You are fine people," he says, "sexy, yet classy, and will most likely be rescued sometime tomorrow afternoon. Nevertheless, I'll be leaving you with a dozen bottles of water because dehydration is a sucker's way of killing."

To Cap, there are distinctly right and wrong ways to conduct a "nautical intervention." It's this unbending adherence to pirating principles that he believes will lead to his future legend.

I respect Cap's ideals, but for me, pirating is just a way to finance my restaurant. Three years ago, when Cap found me, I was working at a little bistro in Crete for a prick of a head chef who took credit for my recipes. Never again. So far, I've saved about ninety thousand dollars, and jewelry worth about fifty thousand. I figure I'll need two hundred and fifty thousand to fund the whole thing.

Cap continues, "I've shared something of myself, I think, in these minutes. You've seen the type of pirate I am, and as a final request I'd ask that each of you suggest a nickname for me: something that could capture the essence of who I am and help me counteract the short memory of Time in the way 'Blackbeard' did for its host, Edward Drummond."

"I don't understand," says a man in tan silk pajamas.

"Please, just leave us alone," another says.

"Kind people," Cap continues, "delight in your fear. Give it a little squeeze. Imagine this time as an extraordinary memory, because it soon will be. Enjoy us! I'm Cap—but I believe there must be a better name out there. This is Bertok. Have you ever seen anyone wider than Bertok? Think about the fine story you'll tell about this someday."

"Don't kill us," says one of the women.

Cap keeps trying to explain how all he wants is a good nickname, but these people are too afraid to understand anything. They snivel and Cap insists they have nothing to snivel about: this is the greatest night of their ho-hum lives. But all his insisting works them up even more and soon one of them, a balding, droopy-eyed man, is in hysterics. Cap gives Daeng a nod and the guy is (mercifully) knocked out by the butt of Daeng's AK-47.

And then his wife is in tears, and Daeng is cursing her for being unappreciative.

"I'm sorry, everyone," Cap says, and he is. He's a peculiar guy, but also utterly sincere and very weepy. "I've tried my best tonight to steal everything you have except your dignity, but I can see I've failed you."

Bertok places an arm around a dejected Cap and leads him back to the ladder.

"Nice one," I say to the crying woman, but of course she's just afraid—didn't mean to upset Cap. Daeng, though, takes out his glass eye and sits directly in front of her, says to look into his skull for forgiveness—he's forever insisting that there's wisdom to be found within the socket—but she doesn't find anything except more fodder for wailing.

And we're out of there.

the haul

Little John guns the *Pertunda* all the way home. There'll be some celebrating tonight. Home is a small uninhabited island about twenty-five miles east of Corfu. Little John is something of a master carpenter and built us five cedar huts with a crapload of fancy adornments like coffered ceilings and herringbone-patterned wood floors. There's no electricity, but he constructed four fire pits that give far better heat than most kitchen burners I've cooked with.

Tonight's haul is five diamond rings, three diamond-encrusted Rolex watches, an emerald necklace, a pair of ruby earrings, some premium navigational equipment, and close to three thousand dollars' worth of euros and American dollars. We lay out the jewelry on a beautiful maple bar top Little John removed from a Swedish yacht a year ago and attached to the makeshift kitchen in Cap's hut. Cap gets first pick. I think all of us respect his discrimination in always picking out the choicest piece. In this case, it's the ruby earrings, which he informs us are cabochon rubies from Burma, very valuable. Bertok goes second, which always pisses off Daeng, and then me, and then Little John, and the order repeats. We split the cash evenly, and when we sell the navigational equipment in Athens, we'll split that too. As for the skin creams and hair toners, they're all Cap's.

While we're recounting our money, Cap reaches into Daeng's pile of jewelry and pulls out a men's diamond ring.

"Mine!" Daeng says.

"Hold on . . . oh, criminy, listen to this." Cap reads the ring's inscription: *I give you my heart.* "We erred taking this ring," Cap says, gravely. "If a woman pledges her heart to some lucky broncobuster, then who are we to snatch that up? We don't burgle hearts, people, only things."

"I would like to barter for that ring," Little John says to Daeng.

"Oh, I couldn't," Daeng says, the salesman. "What sort of a beast would sell a woman's heart? It's worth far more than just money, about a thousand dollars' worth to be exact. In addition to that bejeweled dagger you got on our last heist."

vocabulary

"Heist?" Cap says. "Now what sort of a word is 'heist'?"

"Nautical intervention . . . I meant nautical intervention!"

Cap throws his hands up in disgust: "How do you expect to master this vocation if you can't even master its vocabulary?"

"I'll never get it!" Daeng says, slamming his head against the bar top. "Never! Never!" He continues banging his head and muttering *nautical intervention* with each bang.

Cap stops him just short of drawing blood and tells him that the words we use are just arbitrary symbols and if we can change those symbols we can change the acts they describe. A heist is something awful, but a nautical intervention is an often mystical crossing of paths—a valuable exchange of goods and ideas. Then he pats Daeng on the back, tells him he's proud of his progress and knows he'll continue to grow as a pirate.

"So," Little John says, "a thousand plus the dagger?"

Daeng lifts his head off the bar top to nod. Little John turns to me: "A heart, Mr. Grandma, imagine it. In Athens I give a woman twenty euros and she gives me her rear for ten minutes, but a heart? I didn't think you could buy it."

"I'm not so sure you can," I say.

"Yes," he says. "It's right here," and he gazes at the ring as though it were already satisfying his great need for love.

Little John is the sweetest, gentlest person I've ever known, but his blind attempts at happiness make me feel strangely guilty, as though he were starving and I alone refused to feed him.

le menu

I make quite a dinner that night: beef Wellington and wild mushrooms, a sweet potato gratin with candied ginger, two loaves of sourdough, and steamed island greens with just a splash of lemon and olive oil. As a little gift to Cap, I make the chicken lasagna his grandmother used to make. We eat on the giant banquet table Little John carved in a small clearing behind our huts. The tiki torches surrounding us can't be seen from the sea.

Before we dig in, Cap walks solemnly around the table and says grace: "Sweet Jesus, I haven't seen a spread like this since France, 1983. Her name was Eve and her legs were long, hairy popsicles. Succulent. I'd hold her knees to her chest and spin her around on top of me and she'd yank on my marble bag, curse my family, and try to tear out my eyeballs. Sweet Eve: I still have trouble seeing out of my left eye. Amen."

"Amen," we say.

Bertok goes right for the sweet potatoes, a dish his mother

made when he was a boy. "You!" he shouts, "make the food which makes Bertok want to nuzzle up in warm blanket," and he slaps me on the back and almost knocks me off the bench.

Though I can't imagine Bertok nuzzling up to anything, I'm used to people reacting to my recipes in this way. I've been blessed with the ability to replicate recipes I'm told about, and in doing so, deliver people back to their pasts. I can't explain how I do it, only that memories and flavors are both languages and I'm able to translate one into the other.

Cap, for example, has a real knack for description and has spent hours explaining everything his grandmother's lasagna tasted like and every way it made him feel. He takes a thick slice and cuts it into tiny squares, which he eats one at a time, scattered tears falling down his face and mixing with the sauce.

Daeng picks off the pastry crust from the beef Wellington. He pushes aside the greens and the mushrooms, arranging beef onto blocks of bread and devouring them without tasting. When I have my restaurant, people like him won't be allowed in.

He's a Bugis, from Sulawesi, Indonesia; his people have been legendary pirates and marauders for hundreds of years. The word "bogeyman" is derived from the long-held fear of the Bugis, so it's incumbent on Daeng to be ferocious. In fact, supposedly he was a local hero in his village for foregoing the normal Bugis tradition of being circumcised at age twelve. He waited until he was twenty so that he might "really feel the pain."

Cap treasures this story. He's considering having some touch-up work of his own done as a form of solidarity.

Daeng, despite all this, has never felt up to his responsibility as a modern pirate—has always believed himself an imposter, utterly incompetent and silently mocked by his ancestors and the village elders. For a while, it got so bad that he couldn't even look at his three brothers even though they were pickpockets who aspired to be pirates but didn't have the confidence to pursue it. Daeng left his village and came to America with the dream of riding across the country on horseback, robbing the whole way. He spent two years chasing down cars and trains, aided by a particularly violent pony. Eventually, realizing the land life wasn't for him, he traveled to Greece to apprentice with Cap, who had already established a reputation as a traditionalist.

Daeng is the only thing about these past three years that I regret. Cap tried to explain it once: *Look*, he said, *I allow him a woman once, maybe twice a year, let him kick the crap out of some cocky yachtsman on occasion, but think about how much worse he'd be without my restrictions.*

"Everything is very delicious, Mr. Grandma," Little John says. He's eighteen, from Sri Lanka, though he might as well be from nowhere. He wasn't so much raised as simply left alone, and has no significant memories, either good or bad, about the first sixteen years of his life. We found him a year and a half ago working on a German yacht and he begged us to take him with the rest of the booty. He loves Cap like a father, Bertok, an uncle, Daeng an older brother, and it's since he's joined us that the others have taken to calling me Granny. I'm thirty.

the offer

When the man in the wet suit emerges from the tiki-lit woods, Bertok's machete just appears in his hands and Daeng suddenly has a grenade, pin pulled, ready to throw.

"I'm unarmed," the man says, raising his hands. His wet suit is black, as are his fins, head guard, and face mask. Even his small tank of air is black.

"My crumb, that smells gorgeous," he adds. He has some sort of British accent.

Cap says, "If we'd known you were coming, we could have made extra, but alas . . ."

"Alas," Bertok continues, "all we can offer is stiff kick to groin with foot of machete." Bertok looks at me and grins. I'd recently taught him about personification (he fancies himself something of a poet) and he seems pretty proud of this one.

"Oh, come now," Daeng says, "surely one of us could contribute a bullet in the head for our hungry guest."

The man clutches his gut and shakes with laughter.

"Daeng Dakko, right?" he says. "And Bertok Melles. And I suppose Granny is responsible for all this glorious food. Little John, pleased to make your acquaintance. And you, sir, you must be the great Captain Arthur Trilling. It's truly an honor, sir. I'm a great fan of your work."

He tries to bow to Cap, but Bertok lifts him off the ground with one hand and begins frisking him with the other. "I'm Rick," he says, in midair, "founder and president of International Pirate Exterminators. Perhaps you've seen our Web site?"

I point to the fire pits and the shit shaft and tell him our Ethernet is down. He laughs a bellyful and starts explaining. Most of the pirate catchers in IPE were once pirates themselves, yet are now getting rich by charging corporations a million dollars to retrieve hijacked cargo ships. He's here to offer us a position at IPE, and goes to great length describing the erotic thrill of the bust, the satisfying heft of a brass badge, and the downright whimsy of having so many fancy weapons at one's disposal. "A submarine," he says. "Well, it's what's known as a mini, but still, it has torpedoes."

Torpedoes, Daeng repeats, as though echoing the name of God.

He tells Cap that the fame of the outlaw turned lawman is far greater than that of any simple crook, and says he'd even go so far as to bow out of his contract with the Greek authorities and, instead of throwing our collective asses in jail, award us a signing bonus.

At the mention of jail, I look to Cap and Bertok, but if they heard the threat their faces aren't showing it. Bertok doesn't even seem to be listening, so intent he is on sharpening his machete.

Rick mentions one pirate in particular. "A man who goes by the name of Otis. He's an old associate of yours, Cap, is he not?"

"Is he a giant man?"

"Said to be a seven-footer, but we haven't any photos."

Cap admits to once knowing a very tall Otis. Well, he's quite the crime boss now, Rick explains. In fact, Otis runs the biggest pirating ring in Asia, and if we help "toss his gangly ass in the slammer," there will be quite a bit of money in it for us.

Rick suggests that he's offering us a new life, says to think about it, but not to take too long deciding. He takes a wedge of sweet potato and tells me it could use cinnamon. Bertok sharpens with increased vigor. Rick actually says, "Cheerio," and walks back to the sea, laughing as he goes.

"Great outfit," Cap says, returning to his lasagna. "All that black: very classy."

"What are we going to do?" I say.

Bertok gestures to his machete, says, "Is not too late," but Cap shakes his head.

So we eat. Despite the fact that this is possibly the best beef Wellington I've ever made (getting a perfectly flaky crust is more a matter of divine intervention than any indication of the chef's skill), it's a rather mournful meal, eaten in the silence of the thoughts we're all thinking. Cap finally breaks the silence. He stands, looks each of us in the eye, and says, "We're a team, you hellhounds and I. Bertok, how long we been working together?"

"Years," Bertok says.

"Years! You hear that, people? This Hungarian monstrosity has been saving my behind for an indeterminate number of years." He looks around to make sure we all get it. "And you, Daeng Dakko, miscreant, pestilence, goddamn child beater. My fuck, have you got style! You're a malignance, and if I had any morals at all, you'd be walking the plank faster than I could say 'misanthrope,' 'cause you are one."

Daeng is beaming. He removes his glass eye and shows Cap the socket, something which, no matter how much Little John begs, he'll only do for customers. Cap usually isn't so generous with his compliments, understanding how quickly order and obedience could dissolve.

"Granny," he continues, "you're the warm breast we shimmy up to at night, metaphorically. If you were a nubile young thing, say, sixteen, with firm breasts and a healthy love of pain, I'd shack up with you quicker than you could say 'not so hard,' which you would, eventually, say. You take care of us, Granny.

"And Little J. Christ, what can I say? You're the most uncorrupted human being I've ever met. Fact is, pal, you're better than all us old bastards put together."

Little John, bright red and close to tears, says, "And you, Cap, are even better than that."

"Should we suck each other off now or later?" Daeng asks. "Are we pirates or are we a fucking glee club?"

"Exactly!" Cap replies. "We're pirates and *so what* if we could get a million bucks returning tankers to their corporate berths. Where in the pirate's handbook does it say that lawfulness has anything to do with morality or purity, or with justice? Turning in good honest pirates isn't what I do!"

"It can't really be a million, can it?" Daeng asks.

Bertok says, "If we don't join pirate-catching group, Rick send authorities, and I must to hack them to bits. I am poet; why so many hacking?" He says this with the weariness of someone who's done a lot of hacking in his life. Daeng offers to share in the hacking, and Little John speculates as to whether we'll all be able to share the same prison cell.

"Fellas, fellas," Cap says. "We have to leave. It's as simple as that. We've outgrown Corfu. It's time to join the big leagues."

"Indonesia?" I say.

"Yes, Indonesia! The big leagues are calling, and we're answering that call faster than they can say 'Operation Long-Overdue Notoriety'—faster than they can say 'the prostitutes in Indonesia are so tiny you hardly even notice them.'"

"Am I ready, Cap?" Daeng asks.

"Daeng Dakko, you'll make your people proud."

"Maybe we should just work for Rick," Daeng says. "Lawmen receive generous bribe packages."

"Do you really want a bribe," Cap asks, "or are you just practicing avoidance?"

"But what about our home?" Little John says.

"We'll have to make a new home," Cap says, "somewhere in Jakarta, or maybe the Strait of Malacca."

"No," Little John says. "This is our home," and he gestures to our huts, our small badminton court, to the pit where he's building a sweat lodge.

It's no use: Cap's decided.

the speech

Over the next two days we pack up our things and I begin prepping for a farewell feast. Daeng recites lengthy and often violent positive affirmations at each meal, and Little John recites detailed and often gushing good-byes to every inch of our small island. Cap's put the limit at two suitcases per person. All of us have fancy Italian luggage and a heap of opulent clothes and gadgets we've accumulated in three years of ripping off the wealthy. I even have a diamond Prince Albert that Daeng insisted we take out of sheer barbarity from some poor sap of a yacht captain. In my two suitcases, I manage to fit my set of Henckel knives, all my jewelry and cash, my rolling pin, two Armani suits, and the beautiful silk chef's jacket we nabbed last winter. I think of the future and take clothes that aren't suited to a life of piracy—bright colors, shirts that could tear easily.

I've lived these past three years with no sense of a past or present, always looking forward to the day when I could cook my food for people and do nothing else. Now that it's almost here, I realize how unhappy I've been, spending my days amidst so much fear: the tired, frightened eyes of yacht crews—their fear just another object we have to deal with, like their arms that need binding and their valuables that need stealing. So no, I suppose I'm not a convert to Cap's belief in the beauty of piracy.

And yes, if the money is the same, Rick's offer is tempting, and the thought of going legitimate isn't unappealing. Nevertheless, Cap, Bertok, and Daeng have saved my life so many times, and I don't see how I could go off with the first commando who comes by offering a badge and the threat of jail time.

Besides—God, does this make me an idiot? An egomaniac?—I want to know if the five of us are good enough to make it in the big leagues.

I go all out on the final feast. It's sick, the abundance. I deep-fry prawns in two hundred dollars worth of truffle oil. We eat caviar with soupspoons. Katsu tuna au poivre. I make rémoulade. I make a chestnut beurre blanc. Two kinds of bisque. I stuff foie gras with lobster and sear it in hazelnut oil. Lamb carpaccio with arugula, capers, and roasted yellow peppers. I make three trips into Corfu for supplies. I make bananas Foster. We bust out the hundred-year-old brandy, the vintage champagnes, the burgundies. I make everything I know how to make, knowing that many of these dishes will someday appear on the first menu of Granny's Place (though I imagine the menu as something ephemeral, changing as my customers provide me with their favorite memories, like a diary of many childhoods). We eat so hard, I feel dizzy.

Toward the end of the night, Little John, drunk for the first time in his life, I think, demands that somebody make a speech. "The only thing I can't stand to have taken away is being taken away," he says. "Somebody say something before I shoot myself in the head."

Cap stands, but falls/sits on the ground instead. "Someone else will have to do the honors," he says. Though I'm sure the alcohol had something to do with it, I take a little pride in thinking he's drunk on my food. The three of us look to Bertok, whose tolerance for food and alcohol is inhuman.

He says, "Time to leave Greece. Speech over."

en route

Cap has a friend, Captain O'Brien, who operates a two-hundred-foot casino yacht and it's on this boat that we—and the *Pertunda*, thanks to a crane we brought in from Corfu—make the journey to Jakarta.

It's startling, at first, being surrounded by so many strangers, and the five of us huddle together and watch them (mostly Australians and Scandinavians) out of the corners of our eyes. Crossing the Suez Canal, we collectively snarl at a teenager who tries to start up a conversation. Around the second week, however, Daeng breaks off to gamble and have sex with the ship's prostitutes. Soon Cap and Bertok are hitting golf balls onto Saudi Arabia and Egypt with Captain O'Brien. And then it's just me and Little John, who, with each passing day, gets quieter. The Red Sea isn't at all red, but he stares at it off the aft deck for hours, as though measuring how far we've traveled from home.

I feel for him, knowing how regretfully people move forward, and of course I know all about not letting go; it's the whole point of my cooking. A home can mean all sorts of things in the same way food is far more than just something we chew up in order to survive.

I don't think I've been blessed with many talents. I'm not attractive or charismatic; I don't make people laugh nor do I astound them with my intelligence, yet I have been blessed with the most wonderful gift. My cooking transports people to the one place they most want to return. And everyone has such a place, or a person, or a time, and associated with each of these fantasies, whether people are aware of it or not, are precise combinations of flavor. There is such a thing as a time machine, but try telling that to Little John.

The casino yacht stops wherever Captain O'Brien decides to stop and always some passengers get off and others get on. I don't have any idea how people in, for instance, Djibouti, know to meet us in Djibouti port, or why all these Australians want to travel to Djibouti in the first place, but they do. Sometime around the third week—we've recently passed Cape Gwardafuy, at the tip of Somalia—Rick the commando appears at the rail of the port side deck, same black wet suit, same mask, same tank of air, and heaves himself aboard. He lies sprawled out on his back for a few moments—it must have been a grueling climb—but then pops up abruptly, break-dancer style, and scans the boat.

I run to fetch Cap and Bertok and find them in the bar where Cap is showing off his scars to a couple of Norwegian coeds. His shirt is off and he's in the process of unbuckling his pants. "And this one . . . ," he's saying, but I stop him with the news about Rick. Cap wouldn't kill a messenger, but he'd certainly cry at their feet. Walking out, he asks me about the rumor that Norwegian women have the scent of warm strawberries down there. His little Eve, whom he never tired of dressing and undressing, smelt of nutmeg. "God, I miss you, Eve!" he howls. "But strawberries! Is it true about the strawberries?" I tell him I don't know.

"Then why, why would you interrupt me when I was so close to finding out?" he cries. "How did Rick find us? How could God do this to me?" Then he sighs and hugs me, apologizes for his outburst. The Norwegians must have cast some sort of spell upon him, he says. He takes a moment putting himself back together.

Rick is leaning casually against the railing as though climbing aboard a yacht in the Indian Ocean is nothing out of the ordinary.

"Rick the commando," Cap says. "What a surprise. Awful timing, by the way: I was on the verge of solving one of life's great mysteries."

"Oh, Cap, I'm frightfully sorry," Rick says, sounding oddly sincere. "Shall I come back?" And he actually begins donning his face mask.

"You're here now," Cap says. "What can we do for you?"

"You disappeared," Rick says. He goes on to tell us how hurt he was, and how the hurt quickly turned to anger, then from anger to fury and from fury to madness, and how it was only when he'd found rage that he was able to get back to hurt. He says, "Leaving the island wasn't very obliging, especially as I'd offered you such a damned considerate career change and didn't even have you bloody killed, as was well within my rights as president of International Pirate Exterminators."

"I scoff," Bertok says, and then he does, sort of.

Rick bursts into laughter. He tells us he came here to make generous deals, not threats. He says to round up the others so we can all talk. Cap nods, so I go.

Little John is napping and Daeng is sitting on the floor

beside him polishing his grenades. Shiny weapon parts lie scattered across the floor. I tell Daeng what's up and he and I gently wake up Little John, who buries his head under the covers. Daeng begins tickling him. Eventually, Daeng tosses a grenade into the bed, and it gets buried in the sheets and Daeng and Little John are laughing hysterically, and I'm in the hall waiting for the pin to pop out and the grenade to blow, which, somehow, it doesn't.

Back on deck, Rick is telling Cap and Bertok how perhaps he knew Cap would never turn against Otis and would rather go off to work for him. Perhaps this was my plan all along, he says. Has Cap tried to send Otis a message, by the way? Because he should know that the underground circuit isn't quite so underground anymore.

"Mine is," Cap says.

"Times are changing, Cap. Remember, most of us pirate catchers are ex-pirates. We know all the tricks. Fact is, we're not even too hard on the real pirates, like you or Bertok here."

"My mother gave me name," Bertok says, "say it again, and I fuck you with blade of knife."

"Oh, my goodness, that won't be pleasant, now, will it? I assure you, I don't know what all this hostility is about—it works out smashingly well: Half of us are pirates, the rest are pirate catchers. We are all, as it were, privy to the same body of knowledge and there's money for all. This is a primo ship, by the way. A Captain O'Brien sails it, if I'm correct. Friend of yours, right? Plenty of cash here if some enterprising group of sea dogs should decide to target it.

"Anyway, where was I? Oh, yes, so we at IPE catch a pirate, take the cargo back to the client, and usually this pirate is free to go in a month or two. Fact is, we want the good pirates back out there stirring things up a bit, because, who am I kidding here, these folks are our bread and butter, as it were. Ha ha, ha ha ha! It's these new assholes who need real jail time. These Chinese hotshots—no offense to them of course, grand history, the Chinese, great record of medicines and meditations; rice is gorgeous stuff—but the Chinese, frankly, are perverting the principles of piracy, Cap. They kill entire cargo crews."

"Well," Daeng says, defensively, "cargo crews aren't really that big. What, six, seven people?"

"Sure," Rick says. "Six or seven. But these new pirates don't kill because the crew put up a fight, or even because they just enjoy it: that would be a different story. These guys kill because it's easier to deal with dead crews than to bother putting them on lifeboats. They have no respect for anything. These guys are nothing more than thieves on boats."

"Well, then, they must be stopped!" Cap says.

"Hello?" Rick says. "That's what I'm saying. Someone needs to stop these hacks before they give us all a bad name."

"And you're one of 'us'?" I say.

"Oh, goodness no," Rick says. "I'm a nothing. Don't imagine for a second that I think myself your equal. You folks are shit hot, legendary almost; I'm just a man with a badge. And an army of men working for me. And mansions on six continents."

"And a submarine with torpedoes," Daeng offers.

"Nuclear capability as well, Daeng. Look, I'm not anybody, but you guys are, and Otis is, and these killers are Otis's people, and Cap, you can get us Otis."

"Well, Rick the commando," Cap says, "this is important work you're engaged in. Just the thought of these young bucks giving pirates a bad name—it really burns this old swashbuckler, and by God, if I were a lawman, I'd have them in the slammer quicker than you could say, 'But Cap, I'm asking you to be a lawman,' which I won't, by the way, because that's not what I am."

"And the rest of you?" Rick asks.

"Bertok," Cap says, and gestures to Rick. Bertok picks him up over his head, carries him to the railing—Rick casually lowering his face mask, humming the whole way—and tosses him overboard, face first.

"Oh, Bertok, why?" Daeng says, peering over the side after Rick.

"What you would do with nuclear missile I don't want to know."

"It doesn't sound like a terribly bad offer," Little John

says. "Helping rid the seas of thoughtless cruelty would be, I think, a noble pursuit."

"Go, then," Cap says. "You and Daeng, and Granny if you want, go off with Rick and help make the world a better place—which, by the way, we're already doing with our own work.

"By warning Otis, for example, we're showing the world loyalty. We show them how beautiful a craft can be when performed by masters—teach them through their fear exactly what it is they have to lose; what could be more worthwhile than helping people to recognize the value of their lives?"

"I would never break up this group," Little John says. "I had these feelings and simply wanted to express them."

Cap considers this, then he and Little John do their special handshake. It has knuckle bumping, mock finger pistols, a thumb war, and ends in a bear hug.

the new piracy

The rest of the trip is rather uneventful. The kitchen crew lets me help out and the head chef, a soft-spoken Haitian, even has me plan a few meals. Some nights, after all the work is done, he and I cook for each other, talking sauces and theories of reduction, a buttery roux versus good old-fashioned cornstarch, galangal versus Hawaiian ginger, that sort of thing.

One late night, he tells me the story of his aunt's conch stew, something he's never been able to get right. I make it for him the next day and he cries and tells me I have been blessed with magic powers, tells me that tonight he is a child again and I'm his (now-bearded) aunt. He asks me how I knew she used too much thyme and not enough ground cloves. When I'm told about a dish, I listen to the ingredients, but mostly I pay attention to the way the recipe is conveyed. In this case, it was his scrunched-up face saying that there was too much of one ingredient, and a slight shoulder shrug implying there wasn't enough of another. The cloves were easy, just appeared while he was talking. The thyme, however, was more elusive. I had to replay his facial expressions, hand gestures, his tone of voice.

Periodically, I see Rick slinking in shadows on the yacht. Once I thought I saw him leaping across our boat's wake like a dolphin. I see him corner Daeng and talk rather heatedly with him for some moments before abruptly hurtling back into the sea. One night, I'm sure I hear his voice in Little John's room.

The five of us keep up one ritual: No matter how sore Cap is, or whether Daeng is mad at Bertok, or how much Little John wants to stay in bed pouting, mornings we make time for each other. We sit at a certain table and ridicule the other passengers. Sometimes, I'll have prepared a meal in advance and sometimes we just risk it and eat whatever the morning staff has prepared. If someone's sitting at our special table, Bertok goes over to talk to them, and they're gone in a snap.

On one such morning, we're drinking a beverage I'd created (two parts gin, one part mango pulp, one part soda water, one teaspoon fresh ginger; shake vigorously and serve over ice with a lime wedge and a mint garnish), and we see a group of pirates attacking a yacht about a hundred and fifty yards away. To the untrained eye, it might have just looked like two boats anchored near the Maldives, but Cap spots it right away. Daeng pulls out his Apache binoculars and we all have a look. It's three guys in ski masks and their speedboat is a jalopy tied to the yacht.

Cap eventually takes the Apaches and narrates what's going on, pointing out all the mistakes they're making, which are plenty. They're yelling at the passengers, who aren't even tied up correctly (apparently they're using a clove hitch, a totally inappropriate knot for restraining people). "Policemen yell," Cap says, "to intimidate and dehumanize, but pirates attempt to link us, one to another, through the very things that make us human: fear, love, possession, envy, commerce."

He tells Daeng to go get his sniper rifle just in case these guys decide to start killing. "They're an utterly unskilled menace," he continues. "Who loads booty onto the getaway boat like that!"

I shrug. Soon Daeng comes back with the gun draped under a blanket. On his command, Daeng should blow off the legs of the shortest pirate. This is probably his dream task: a Cap-authorized sniper shot to the knees. He never gets to take the shot. The pirates don't kill anyone, and soon speed away, leaving a trail of gray exhaust in their wake.

Cap lowers the binoculars and tells us that in all his years as a pirate, he's never seen such messy, incompetent work. "How can pirates like this exist?" he asks, and then answers it himself. "There's no real danger to piracy because nobody resists anymore. People either expect the law to show up or know their stuff is insured, anyway, so why bother warding off attackers. There's too much damn acquiescence, not enough at stake, and so any asshole with a boat and a gun can call himself a pirate. They've made a mockery of my life's work," he says, gesturing to the sea and then the sky, a gesture of pleading, though I'm not sure to whom, or for what.

Later that day, after a drop-off and pickup at the Nicobar Islands, I'm in my room writing down a recipe for a grape-fruit and avocado salad with a lime-and-ginger dressing—I had a dream about such a salad last night—and Rick crawls out from under my bunk, apologizes for startling me, and starts in on whether or not I fancy helping him bring down Otis. He promises nothing will happen to any of us, and that he'll be happy to donate some prime real estate in the swanky part of Jakarta where I can open my restaurant. He and his associates own all sorts of land and I can have my pick of the litter.

He's offering me the only thing in this life I know I want, so I focus on the water he's dripping all over my floor. Who knows how he slipped in undetected?

Even without Rick, I think they all knew that someday our group would break up, and that, most likely, I'd be the first to leave.

"I'll think about it," I say.

"Oh, brilliant!" he responds. "Think real hard about it. Because when I do manage to entice one of you, who are pirates after all, to turn against Otis, then certainly you'd want to be on the right team when his booty gets divvied up."

landfall

We arrive at Jakarta's Sunda Kelapa port early in the morning, six weeks after leaving Corfu. It smells of fish and fuel, and the water and sky are a gloomy, defecatory brown. I remember a time when I probably couldn't have said what country Jakarta was in, let alone known that it was the epicenter of modern piracy—or that such a thing even existed. According to Cap, Indonesia is the capital of piracy because their laws so clearly favor us. The crews of cargo ships are prohibited from carrying guns, and when the Japanese government began complaining about their ships being hijacked by pirates, the Indonesians said they couldn't afford more patrol boats. The Japanese offered to send in armed boats of their own, but Indonesia refused, claiming it would be a breach of their sovereignty.

A crane lifts the *Pertunda* off the yacht and into the water. We shake hands with Captain O'Brien, the chef hands me a kitchen rag he's embroidered with our initials and the initials of his aunt, and we grab our suitcases and disembark.

It's remarkably comforting: the five us again aboard the *Pertunda*. Daeng inhales the musty, polluted air, yells out that Indonesia's most hardcore son has returned, and Cap announces that the warm-strawberry theory has been officially debunked.

Around noon, two of Otis's associates come knocking. Daeng acts as translator; I can't imagine anyone I'd trust less.

Daeng informs us, "They claim to want to take us to Otis, but I believe they will lead us to some forsaken place where we will be killed and then dismembered."

"What makes you believe that?" I ask.

"The shorter one," Daeng whispers, "has fang-like teeth and I believe he is a Jew. Jews are known killers."

"Jews don't have bad teeth," I say.

"Otis and I experimented orally on each other as teenagers," Cap says. "Lead me to Otis. Otis is my man."

While Daeng explains this to the two men, Cap says, to no one in particular, "Blackbeard was bisexual, you know."

Somebody needs to stay with the boat and guard our ten suitcases, so we arm Little John to the teeth. Daeng even instructs him in how to use his rocket-propelled grenade launcher. "With this button you slaughter," Daeng explains.

"With this button I slaughter," Little John repeats. He sounds as though he'd happily give away all of his money and jewels in order to avoid slaughter.

"No matter what happens," I whisper, "don't hurt anyone."

"Oh, thank you, Mr. Grandma," he whispers back, relieved, "thank you!"

the lowdown

We meet Otis in an empty back room of a ritzy bar, a mile or so away from downtown Jakarta. Enormous men with AK-47s lurk in corners. Otis is probably the tallest person in the world.

"Captain Arthur Trilling, you old child molester, you!" he thunders and wraps up Cap in all those lanky limbs.

"Otis, you old hound dog, you rice-eating mooncalf, you Harlem Globetrotter in disguise!"

"Let me look at you, Arthur," Otis says, placing his enormous hands on Cap's shoulders. "A little older and a little uglier, but otherwise, the same. A perfect blight on the civilized world!" They embrace again. These two are perfect together.

"And you," Cap says, "if I hadn't lost my favorite testicle to a murderous bull shark in the Gulf of Guinea, I'd have you on display at the Jakarta zoo quicker than you could say,

'Don't feed the animals,' which they wouldn't, because there'd be signs warning against it, and heavy fines."

This exchange, somehow, continues for some time. Bertok, Daeng, and I sit down at a booth and soon a tiny waitress in tight black appears with warm snifters of cognac. I say to Bertok, "You think you could take somebody that tall?"

"Once—I was very drunk—I get into fistfight with Cap's baby rhinoceros. It weighs thousand pounds, at least, tries to crush me to death, but in time I knock it out."

"You can't be serious," I say.

"I lost fifty euros on that fight," Daeng says.

Daeng's been talking to the waitress, and he says something that makes her storm off. She returns with Cap and Otis, and Otis says, "I'm sure I didn't just hear you say what I think I just heard you say."

"I asked for some suck and blow," Daeng says. "Is that such an awful thing?"

"If you ever speak to my wife like that again, I'll have you killed and thrown into the biggest hole you'll ever see."

"Which you won't, see that is, because you'll be deceased," Cap says. Then, "Fellas, fellas, all these death threats and propositioning of wives are all fine and good, but maybe it's best we get down to business."

Daeng and Otis say a few angry-sounding words in Indonesian, and then Otis has a seat. He expresses how honored he'd be if we'd intercept a Dutch cargo ship for him in the Strait of Malacca. The ship is carrying five million dollars' worth of sugar. To me that seems unfathomable. We're to commandeer the ship, set the crew afloat on rafts, and pilot it to the Chinese port of Beihai, where Otis's men will unload it, repaint it, and eventually sell it.

Cap does know how to pilot a cargo ship, does he not? Oh, yes, Cap assures him, he's piloted his share of ships.

We'll need a few more men with us, Otis says, and offers us the armed guys in the corners. Though none of us whoops when he tells us the job pays four hundred thousand American dollars, I know I sure want to. The most we've ever taken in one night is eight thousand cash and a couple grand worth of jewelry. With my share of the payment (and maybe a small loan), I'll have just enough to open my restaurant.

Cap thanks him for the kind offer and explains how the International Pirate Exterminators are on a quest to shut Otis down.

At this, Otis laughs, a booming laugh. "Rick!" he finally says, "Rick is a liar and a murderer. Don't believe anything he says." He explains how IPE hires its own pirates who are usually under orders to kill the crews of ships they attack, and then Rick has other IPE members apprehend them and either bribe for their release or, more often, just kill them so he won't have to pay them.

If Otis is telling the truth, then we were right to come here. If he's lying, maybe Rick's offer of legitimacy isn't such a bad one. I look at Bertok, who shrugs.

"Keep clear of Rick and the rest of IPE," Otis says, "but

don't worry about them either." They're fags, he says, and he'll take care of them.

Who knows what to think?

"So," Otis says. "Do we have a deal?"

"We do," Cap says, "provided we can take on Daeng's brothers as the extra men in our team. They don't have a lot of experience, but they come from good blood."

Daeng has about the biggest smile I've ever seen. It doesn't suit him.

Otis gives us the lowdown: When we intercept (three days), precisely where in the Phillip Channel we should strike, how many crew members the cargo ship will have (eight to twelve), how fast they'll be traveling (eight knots). Afterwards, we would do well to lie low for a month or so. He says he usually pays in full upon delivery, but since Cap is such a pal, would we like some of the money now?

"Yes," we say. "We would like some money."

"Are you armed?" he asks. We point to Bertok.

"I am shot eleven times," Bertok says, bored. "Bullets don't hurt much."

Otis nods his head toward one of the corner thugs, who quickly produces a cardboard box with one hundred thousand dollars in it.

Cap and Otis embrace a few more times, Bertok and I shake his hand, Otis lets Daeng know how many times he would have been killed already were he not an associate of Cap, and we leave.

Back at the boat, Little John wants details. The five of us lie on the deck like old times and listen to his excitement. *How tall was Otis really? Were he and Cap happy to see each other?* I tell him everything I can remember, but he wants more. *What was the first thing they said to one another?* He asks Bertok if he was jealous seeing Cap with an even older friend than he was. Bertok laughs and tells the story of beating Cap's rhino.

"That's a beautiful story," Little John says. "You beat his rhinoceros to unconsciousness yet the two of you are still close. What an exquisite thing friendship is."

"I loved that rhino," Cap says.

"It provoked me," Bertok says.

"Otis is a big fucking asshole with no sense of common animal desires!" Daeng declares.

"Daeng tried to fuck his wife," I explain.

"He spoke to me as if I were a child. When my brothers get here, we will take care of him."

"Gadzooks," Cap says, "that's a brawl I'd love to see— you four little hairy men against that great beast Otis— love to see it! But so we understand each other, this fight of yours isn't to take place until our job is done and I'm knee deep in money and Eve's shaved pubis. You understand that, right?"

"I understand that Otis is a great bitch who must pay."

"Well, that's perfectly reasonable," Cap says, "but also understand that if you do anything to wreck this nautical intervention, I'll have you anchored to the bottom of the sea faster than—"

"Faster than," Bertok says, "you can say, 'Bertok, pulverize this piece of shit, weigh him down with one-hundred-seventy-five-pound metal bar, and dump cadaver overboard.'"

"That hurts," Daeng says. "What about all that stuff about us being a family and me being a malignance? Now, suddenly I'm a piece of shit?"

"We are a family," Cap says. "It's just that I'm the ruthless patriarch of this family and Bertok is the hangman."

"Perhaps a family should not have a ruthless male figure and a hangman," Little John says.

"Well said, Little J. But this one does."

Bertok claps Daeng on the back to show him there's no hard feelings, but he looks like a kid who's just dropped his last cookie. Little John gives Daeng a hug and says, "If you want, you could reinstruct me on the most lethal methods of annihilating human beings. That always makes you feel better." Daeng pouts, but soon they're sharpening the edges of throwing stars, and discussing the proper velocity for tossing grenades.

confession

Even though it's just a thirty-seven-footer, we decide to spend the three nights until the nautical intervention aboard the *Pertunda*. It won't be comfortable, but none of us feels safe walking the streets of Jakarta with our precious suitcases—no matter how many times Bertok has been shot. We sleep in shifts so there's always two of us on watch.

The first night, Little John makes a confession. The two of us are supposed to be on guard, but are actually fishing. I'd never eat anything caught in this water, but we used to fish on our island, and when he'd suggested it for "old times' sake," I couldn't turn him down. He tells me all the things he'd almost done to sabotage our departure from the island—how he considered cutting a hole in the bottom of the *Pertunda*, or simply setting it afloat. If he burned everyone's suitcases full of money, wouldn't we have had to stay together to earn more? And today, he tells me, while we were with Otis, he was very close to just taking the boat and leaving.

"Why are you telling me this?"

"I told Cap as well."

"What did he say?"

"He said a mutiny is punishable by death. I also told Daeng, and he said if I stole from him he'd cut off my head and perform a particularly filthy act into my neck. Bertok said he would have cried as he was pulling my limbs from my body. It's strange to me, Mr. Grandma, that in trying to keep this family together I'm being threatened with so much death."

"How would you leaving help to keep us together?"

"You wouldn't be able to complete the last job . . . I don't know, maybe if I were gone, you'd see how terrible it is for us to live apart."

"It's just me that's leaving," I say. "You guys will still be together."

"No. I believe this cargo ship will be the end of us. We'll separate rather than build a new home together."

Though I hadn't really thought about it, his words ring true. Still, I tell him he's wrong—explain that we're a family and the connections between us can't simply be cut, even if one of us does leave. My own words also ring true, so I'm not sure what to think.

loyalty

Daeng Dakko's three brothers show up the next day; they're like a single beast sharing one Dakko brain. At first, the brothers seem content to stare at Daeng, whom they obviously adore, but soon the four of them are holding ludicrous competitions to see who can withstand the most pain. By the end of the day, their arms and legs are butchered with lighter burns and knife cuts spelling out idiot mottoes like "Fuck till I puke," and Ram—I think that's his name—is positively strutting because he was able to tap a pin two centimeters under his thumbnail, a full centimeter further than the next closest Dakko.

At night, Daeng lectures them about the dos and don'ts of pirating, and though I've never heard Bugis before, it sure sounds like a language pirates might use—its grunts and rolls similar to the pitch and roll of a boat in rough seas. Daeng shows them his somersault and recites Cap's speeches (taking on Cap's mournful gaze); he mimics me defending myself with a rolling pin, and Bertok picking people up and then smashing them to the ground. Little John frowns at the smashing, and Daeng, I think, explains to his brothers that Little John has been quite the Sad Sally since we left the island.

The brothers lean in. They laugh at nothing. This is their big brother teaching them something and they don't want to miss a word. Cap watches like a proud parent, knowing, I suppose, that Daeng is teaching them everything Cap himself spent so long imparting.

That night, Bertok and I on guard: We're discussing the difference between simile and metaphor. He'd again confessed his desire to lock himself in the hold of the *Pertunda* and just write write write. I'm no writer, but I remember some of the definitions from school. "Okay, so in the sentence 'Artie barked like a dog, whereas Artie himself was a life unleashed' what's the simile and what's the metaphor?"

Bertok mutters, "It's Rick," and walks down the dock toward a shadowy figure.

"Gentlemen," Rick says. He's got the same wet suit on, same tank of air, black goggles.

"Don't you have any regular clothes?" I say.

"A joke, right? At my expense! Perfect. Ha, ha, ha, ha, ha! I like to think of this as my quick-getaway outfit."

"Rats often slink away," Bertok says.

"Yes, good one, Bertok! Ha, ha ha! Rick the rat at your service. I'm more of a slithering eel, I suppose. Because of the water. You get it, don't you? Lovely machete, by the way, Bertok. You keep it shining just so."

"I shine it like the fireman puts out flames of panic. Simile and metaphor."

Rick ignores this. I do as well since I'm not sure either of those was correct. Rick says it isn't too late to join his team. He knows Otis is planning something.

I say, "Are you sure this Otis even exists? That can't be an Indonesian name."

"What a brilliant question, Granny. How many nights have I lain awake wondering that same thing? Maybe Otis is just a name people came up with to throw me off their trail—some bloke's dog perhaps. Gosh, that would be a hoot, eh? Me devoting ten years of what was once an outright cheery life to bringing down a Dalmatian or even a teacup poodle. Ha, ha! Ha, ha, ha!"

It occurs to me that Rick is probably insane.

He brings in religion, compares his search for Otis to a search for God. He goes on and on. He goes on and on some more. I watch Bertok trim his fingernails with his machete.

"A million dollars," he finally says. He'll give us a million dollars to deliver him Otis, whether or not Otis is fictional.

That's five hundred grand each, or two hundred grand if we decide to split it with the rest of the group. We can either work with him after that, or not.

There's a bit of a ruckus up the dock and we see three men running toward us. "Well, I must be going, chaps," Rick says, putting on his mask. "Please consider the offer."

And then he's gone, a backward plunge into the black water. The three men (Otis's guards?) point flashlights and automatics into the water. "Fuckeeng Reek," they say to us, their lights and guns pointing in all directions, but Rick is nowhere.

The next day, the day before the heist, we have a minor crisis. Daeng's apparently told his brothers about Otis threatening him and they've made it clear that the only honorable thing to do is kill him. Why the fuck are we protecting him, Daeng wants to know. Two days ago, Rick offered him half a million dollars to turn in Otis. Why shouldn't he?

Daeng has sent his brothers off for the day, so it's the five of us sitting on the *Pertunda* snacking on a peanut, sesame seed, and honey mix I roasted on a hotplate we keep on board. "He offered Bertok and me a million," I say.

"Honor is very important in Bugis culture," Daeng says, "and Otis has taken a very large dump all over mine. I propose we go to Otis's bar, kill his guards, kill him, then set up and kill Rick. Take all the loot and buy ourselves a small country somewhere and fill it with slaves. Maybe kill all the pirate catchers as a powerful message to others."

"Any sort of message you have in mind?" I say.

"You are shameful animal," Bertok says.

"What?" Daeng says, "I'm pragmatic!"

"You belong in diminutive cage, case closed."

"But a million dollars," I say, "just for telling Rick about Otis."

"You'd just take the money and leave us," Little John says. "We'd never see you again unless we visited your restaurant."

"Oh, come on, Little John," I say.

"Kill Granny, too, if we have to," Daeng says, who's somewhat out of control at this point and is taking out and then putting in his glass eye over and over.

"Let's just go," Little John pleads. "Back to our island— to Greece. I could build a rudimentary hot tub. We could bring Eve to live with us, get Daeng a slave. We'd all be together."

"Fellas, fellas," Cap says. "What's this really about?" He stands and begins pacing. Is this Daeng genuinely wanting to cause Otis some good, honest pain, he asks, or is it simply a case of Daeng being afraid of letting his brothers down: of failing as both a tough guy and as a pirate? Daeng acknowledges that maybe he's both afraid *and* really wants to hurt Otis. Little John confesses that he, too, is a bit afraid. A cargo ship, after all, seems fundamentally different from a yacht.

Cap sighs and then sighs again. "My goodness, is fear powerful," he says. "Fellas, we're on the cusp of our most elegant nautical intervention. Five million bucks worth of sugar. I can almost hear future generations singing about this event or memorializing it in some sort of blockbuster-caliber film. Imagine the sort of tales that'll be told about the great pirate Cap and his decision to value loyalty over a sizable booty. If only Homer were around to tell it! Because this is about loyalty, people. And purity. And faith, I think. Don't you see? All the trust we've built up in our years together is being tested right now: You don't owe "your culture" any loyalty, Daeng, you owe it to each of us, and we to you. This is what I've been teaching you. This is exactly why I'm here!

"My code, the sacrifices I've made, all the long, hot hours; this moment is precisely where my whole life has led me. And what a feeling, fellas. What a delicious feeling to know I'm doing what I'm supposed to be doing."

He stands there, eyes closed, enjoying his delicious feeling. He asks if Daeng knows what he should be doing.

"I'm a pirate," Daeng says. "I'm learning to be a better pirate and someday I'll be the teacher you've been to me."

"Yes, by God! Yes! And a pirate doesn't kill seven-foot crime bosses; a pirate engages in the art of piracy. Granny, do you know why you're here?"

"I'm here because people have to eat, and only an animal would use sesame seeds without first toasting them."

"Wrong. Engaging, but wrong. You're here for the same reason a cut hand feels better after your mother kisses it, the reason homemade chicken soup heals a cold; you're here because we were all once breastfed, and we miss it."

"My teats are dry," I say.

"I'm serious," he says. "I'm saying something downright momentous and you're missing me entirely."

"I hear you," I say.

"Your lasagna means more to me than you'll ever know." He grabs me by the shoulders and looks close to tears. He cries a lot for a pirate, something I find very endearing.

"We can't go back to Greece, fellas. Our little island life, well, that life ended the moment Rick showed up. This is our life now, and we can either screw each other over, or not. God, I love this! All the loot in Indonesia on the line, and it comes down to loyalty. Loyalty to Otis, to piracy, loyalty to each other."

Well, there's hugs, vows exchanged, talk of Otis being the uncle we've banded together to protect. Honestly, though, I'm thinking about how much kitchen equipment Rick's money would get me, Daeng still seems undecided, and Little John looks depressed and somewhat unpredictable. Also, I'm a bit worried about what Rick might do when he realizes we've abandoned him again.

Cap, however, is a man possessed with certainty—he glows with it—and maybe his is enough for all of us.

one creature, one purpose

Cap insists we fill up on carbs because he likens piracy to marathon running. He somehow finds pancakes and fried potatoes and brings them back on board. He also brings sealable plastic bags, which he suggests we fill with our money, and strap to our bodies in case we have to leap overboard, or in case Little John is apprehended aboard the *Pertunda*. Not very encouraging.

The eight of us huddle on the boat, eating and going over the plan one last time. Daeng shows Cap the knot he'll use on the rope ladder. Little John does throat exercises to help him project his sperm whale call. Bertok naps. It's not exactly nervousness I feel, it's more a sense that this is it. This one job, if we do it correctly, will be the last thing I'll ever have to do for money again, as though it's less sugar that we're stealing today so much as time.

At midnight, we leave Sunda Kelapa port for the three-and-a-half-hour trip to the Phillip Channel. About three hours in, we make the crossing into the Strait of Malacca. "Thirty minutes, people," Cap says. "I know it's a bit early, but I'm going to go ahead and give the command for silence."

Daeng explains the command to his brothers, who begin donning black masks and pulling out far too many guns and knives from duffel bags and stuffing them into holsters attached all over their bodies. The Dakkos are a well-armed family.

"Tonight, I will make Blackbeard himself proud," Daeng says, and Cap hugs him.

It's pitch black except for the green glow of our navigation system. I take a deep breath and run my hand over the warm wood of my rolling pin. My lucky charm. In the distance, I see the lights of the cargo ship like flashing animal eyes.

Bertok begins poking around his back with a machete. "My God, I'm going to miss that," Little John whispers, reaching over to scratch the itch. Soon I can make out the outline of the sugar ship, huge and growing huger as we travel in opposite directions toward our respective futures, ours to rob them, theirs to be robbed. I can hear that the eight of us have begun to inhale and exhale together, a good sign, as though we're one creature with one purpose.

the intervention

Daeng climbs aboard first, something his brothers seem infinitely proud of, and, when he's attached the rope ladder to the rail of the ship, the rest of us climb aboard, too. Right away things feel wrong. Too quiet, less like silence than the sound of being waited for.

We take cover behind freight boxes and wait as well, though we don't know for what. The light sounds of moving water, the silver glow of moonlight. And then . . . a sperm whale call, the only sperm whale within a thousand miles.

Then shots.

The one thing to avoid at all costs, Cap often said, was a firefight. We weren't soldiers who killed indiscriminately, and our customers weren't our enemies. In the case of a firefight, we were to retreat.

The whale call, however, means that patrol boats are coming, and when I look down, they already have Little John in cuffs.

There are lots of boats and all of them have IPE written across their sides in broad red strokes. Little John keeps crying out his whale call, keeps warning us, and it's the first time I notice how mournful the whale's call is, as though it's a song constructed of tears.

Bertok cuts the ladder to keep IPE from climbing aboard; we have nowhere to go. Daeng and his brothers return fire, and Cap tries to restrain them, to tell them it's over.

"It isn't over yet," Bertok says, advancing forward.

One of Daeng's brothers takes the first hit, his left arm hanging limply, blood steadily dripping to the ground. Then Bertok gets a bullet in the bicep. He points to it, happy as a kid pointing to a spider he's found.

Cap stands up. Waving his hands above his head, he walks out into no-man's land. And everything just stops. Nobody fires a bullet. He paces in the area between us and them for a full minute, and it's obvious he's preparing a speech of our surrender. But it won't just be about us; it'll be a speech about the role of piracy in the modern world, about devoting yourself to a craft—a speech about believing so hard in something that your conviction can stop bullets. He opens his mouth.

Daeng, I think, fires first, and that fire is returned. Cap's body jerks back and forth, blood spraying in all directions. He staggers backwards and falls overboard.

Daeng stands, throws a handful of grenades, and is shot in the chest. He emits the loudest fart I've ever heard, and is shot in the thigh. He plucks his glass eye from the socket and throws that, then another grenade, then a jury-rigged boomerang with a metal spike at the end. Then his head sort of explodes, and he crumbles. His brothers rush forward, screaming and shooting, but when I take a peek, they're lying ten yards ahead, bleeding, on top of one another.

So it is just Bertok and me, against two or three of them. Bertok is covered in blood but otherwise seems fine.

A shot to the head doesn't make him cry out; he simply curls up like he's decided to take a nap.

I pick up his gun and empty it. I hear a grunt across the way, as though I've shot someone. I wait, but nothing happens. There seems to be no one left, only silence, except for the IPE boats chugging around looking for a way to board.

I close my eyes and reach under Bertok's shirt, his skin sticky and hot, and find his two sealed plastic bags of money, jewels, and poems. I crawl over to Daeng's body, again close my eyes, and reach under his shirt until I find his sealed bags. My arms are covered in blood. I run below deck and don't stop until I get to the galley.

I hide in the grease trap. It's pitch black, silent, and I'm utterly engulfed by the scent of generic Chinese food. Soon, there's the steady sloshing of the ship's movement. Days pass, or maybe just hours. I can hardly feel my body, submersed in warm oil. The world I inhabit is frictionless.

When I no longer hear men searching about or feel the movement of the ship, I come out. The coast is clear.

ACKNOWLEDGMENTS

MY SINCERE GRATITUDE to the many hardworking editors who were kind enough to publish my work, especially Anna Shearer at *Meridian* and Howard Junker at ZYZYVVA.

Thanks, Bud, for naming the book. Thank you to Irini Spanidou, an honest, brilliant, and cherished teacher, writer, and friend. I am indebted to all my friends who were forced to read the foulest drafts of these stories, and were generous enough to help me rather than just slugging me in the groin.

Michelle Wildgen is the most astute, thorough, and hilarious book editor ever. Her efforts have improved this book in innumberable ways. Thanks to my heroic, meticulous, and superb agent, Alex Glass. Grateful thanks to everyone at Tin House Books.

These stories could not have been written without my four amazing parents, my three adorable idiot brothers, and my sister, Nicole. Wholehearted thanks to the Chapis family.

I am most grateful to Jennifer, for her invaluable comments on these stories, for her sweetness, her dead-sexiness, and for her love.